SHOW RED FOR DANGER

Show Red for Danger

A Captain Heimrich Mystery

BY

RICHARD AND FRANCES
LOCKRIDGE

J. B. LIPPINCOTT COMPANY
Philadelphia   New York

SHOW RED FOR DANGER

I

FROM WHERE THEY sat they could see the Hudson. It was wide and quiet and far below them; there was haze to the west and the late sun, sinking into haze, was dimmed, so that there was a golden cast in the slanting light. The distant water of the river held the faintly golden hue.

They sat on a wide chaise on the terrace of a house which once had been a barn, and still somewhat resembled a barn. A big ash tree shaded them and Heimrich looked up into its branches. Pruned now. It had badly needed pruning when he had first seen it, noting its need casually, with the instinctively assaying eye of a country-man. A good many things had happened in the past two years or so—trees pruned and a driveway mended, so that it might be said that minor good had come of major evil. Murder is always evil, in Heimrich's view, even if the victim can be said to have asked for it. As, many in the town felt, Orville Phipps had asked. So— A long time ago. Over and done with, and he here.

He turned his head slightly and looked at Susan Faye—at the clear line of her thin face, at the widely set gray eyes, fixed now on the distant river. Thinking of what, he wondered. Of days even longer ago? Of a younger man long dead who once had shared this terrace with her, looked down with her at the great river? It was likely. Much too likely.

Her face had been far too thin when he had first seen it, and thought, absently, that she was not pretty—that nobody could really call her pretty—but that it was fun to look at her. Her face was still thin, the cheeks still faintly hollowed. But there was repose in her face now, he thought, and she did not, at any rate, look so tired—

[7]

so tired and strained. An improvement, he thought, which could be credited to the late Mr. Phipps who had—Heimrich thought it must have been inadvertently—left a second cousin ten thousand dollars. Hence a fabric shop, hence a pruned ash tree, hence relaxation in a face. A face now very dear.

A long girl—long brown legs, wide shoulders, slender feet in sandals. A girl most delectable, pretty or not; a girl of lightness and grace compact. Heimrich sighed, silently, and regarded himself—looked down himself. Certainly not light; a length of great and evident solidity. Not fat—he would give himself that. Merely heavy. In all respects heavy, Heimrich thought of himself. Too heavy for such grace; his hands too square and hard to touch, to imprison, quicksilver.

Comfortable to be with, he thought, and gave himself that, could not deny himself that. She found him so. That much was evident; he was not wrong about that. Comfortable. Like—like an older brother. Or, possibly, an uncle. He checked his descent into melancholy; into, he had to admit, self-pity. He was older—older as well as heavier. But not that much older. Twelve years, or thereabouts.

She had kissed him when he came half an hour ago—came to sit on the terrace with her, have a drink with her; take her, in due time, to dinner. And it was by no means the first time. Once or twice he had thought, briefly— He turned the thought off. Young women kiss brothers.

He's in it again, Susan Faye thought, regarding the distant Hudson. Whatever will I do with him? It was in a way touching. It was also not a little exasperating. The trouble with them, Susan thought, is that they think too much. Or think they think. Take everything into account, including relative ages. As if one could, or as if there were any point to it. And there was nothing she could do or, at any rate, would do. Beyond what she had done, and if that had not been enough—well. The great oaf.

[8]

Does he think we break? Susan thought, and almost at once corrected the thought. She had no doubt, none whatever, that Merton Heimrich had learned from adequate experience that women are not especially breakable. What it comes to (she thought) is that for one reason and another he puts me in a special category. "Breakable. Handle With Care." Or do not handle at all. She supposed, in honesty, that she should find this flattering. Instead of damned annoying. The great oaf!

Different from others. Too special—all right, call it "precious"— for his clumsy hands. Which were not that, except in his mind. Damn, Susan Faye thought. A lovely, lazy afternoon and a man in the doldrums. And, to some degree, my fault. I should never have shown him that picture of big Michael. Things were going fine until I did that.

She could think now of big Michael, a husband killed in war, with no special pain, with only a kind of soft sadness—a sadness belonging to another life, almost to another woman; a brief sad poem, echoing gently in the mind; there to be recalled but there also to be forgotten. It wasn't bright of me, she thought—not bright at all to, having come on a photograph while in search of something else, have said, "This is a picture of Michael," and held it out to Merton Heimrich. (Why does he hate his own given name so much? Why isn't the great oaf simple and uncomplex, the way a big man—and a policeman to boot—ought to be?) Why was I that half-witted? It set us back almost to the beginning. Damn!

She could herself look now at a picture of big Michael and feel only the sad sweetness of the poem, written down, remembered. And Michael would not, of course, be now as young as he had been when the picture was taken—probably not so darkly handsome, so slimly tall. The great oaf might realize that.

"He was a very handsome man," Heimrich had said, those months ago, and handed the photograph back. And, of course, gone into "it" again. She knew the symptoms now; had known them for a long time. He had looked at the picture of Michael and seen her and Michael together, as they had been briefly, long ago—seen youth shared, and the long smooth bodies of youth and—damn the man!

He was looking at her now. She did not need to turn her head to know that. Looking at her and thinking he was too old for her and too heavy in mind and body. When all he had to do was to turn to her, and to lips that waited. And were, come to that, getting damn tired of waiting.

He knew they waited, she thought. That was the trouble. He knew but he didn't believe. What I should do, she thought, is to get sunburned, and peel. Very unbecomingly. Then he'd quit thinking—and you *are* a conceited filly, aren't you? For all you know—

In a few minutes, Susan Faye thought, we'll both be weeping into our beer. If we had beer to weep into. How can two perfectly normal people get so bollixed up about nothing? Or, as it turns out, about everything?

"What time is it getting to be?" Susan Faye asked.

Heimrich looked. It was getting to be on toward six. Six of a July afternoon, a Saturday afternoon.

Their voices were low, but were heard. There was a soft rubbing sound under the chaise, and a little scratching. A very large dog came out from under the chaise; came out in segments. It was inconceivable that he could have been under the chaise. There was evidently no room under any chaise for so much dog. He could not have got under it; the chaise must have been built over him.

He was a Great Dane, massive even for his breed. He stretched ponderously, he turned around and sat down—on his tail—and looked at them. He looked at them through tremendous brown eyes, and seemed to weep.

"He's gone to camp, Colonel," Susan Faye said. "You know that. You drove up with us."

Colonel put his tongue out, and wept with his tongue.

"Six weeks, Colonel," Heimrich said. "You can stand it for six weeks."

Colonel looked at Heimrich. He extended forelegs in front of him and collapsed, with a thud. That was his way of lying down. He put his great head on his enormous feet and a mammoth sigh ran through his body.

"You," Susan Faye said, "are a most depressing dog."

Colonel made no reply. All hope was evidently abandoned.

"He does," Susan said, more or less in defense, "have his enthusiasms. Whatever he looks like. The boy, of course—most of all the boy. But now and then, somebody else. Heaven knows how he picks but he can be very demonstrative. Almost like a puppy."

Colonel said nothing, but moaned slightly. Heimrich said, "Hm-mm."

Suppose, Susan Faye thought, I just said, "I love you, you great oaf. I'll marry you tomorrow. And you're not clumsy and I won't break and we would have a fine time together and it would be very good for both of us. And as for a few years' difference in our ages— poof. Poof and phooey. And—"

"Why," Susan Faye said, "don't you make us another drink? We've time for a short one before—you don't mind stopping by Brian's, really? I told him you might be with me."

"Of course not," Heimrich said, and swung himself off the chaise, moving with great definition, great economy and thinking that he probably looked rather like a hippopotamus. He went across the terrace toward the house and she turned and watched him. A tall, solid man who nevertheless moved lightly. And hadn't the faintest idea he did.

"What shall I do about him?" Susan asked the big dog. The big dog sighed. "You're probably right," Susan said and lighted a cigarette.

Heimrich came out with short (presumably) gin-and-tonics on much ice. He sat on the side of the chaise, facing her. He held a drink out to her and she took it in a slim, brown hand. The hand which relinquished the glass to hers was brown, too, and rather square and evidently very strong. Didn't the great oaf know what to do with hands like—

"Michael mind leaving all the excitement?" Heimrich said, speaking quickly, matter-of-factly, and acutely conscious of the slender tanned legs within touch. He put his free hand in his jacket pocket.

All right, Susan thought. Any way you want it, for now. But don't think—

"It isn't," she said, "as if they were cowboys. I pointed Mr. Dale out to Michael in front of Hopkins' and said, 'That's Francis Dale, the movie actor' and you know what he said? He said, 'All right. Can I have a Coke?' It's the lack of horses, I suppose. And six-shooters. In civvies—just a man to Michael. And an old one."

And there, she thought, I go again. I deserve what I get—what I don't get.

"Dale was in the taproom when I came through," Heimrich said, and did not need to identify the taproom, since there was only one thereabouts which might be graced by Mr. Francis Dale. "Wearing a green velvet coat and an embroidered waistcoat and knee-breeches. And slippers with silver buckles. And drinking what looked like a Bloody Mary."

"And," Susan said, "handsome as hell. And—he must be in his fifties."

Heimrich supposed so. He said that he thought young Michael might have liked the green velvet coat.

"Makes a nice change," Susan Faye admitted, and sipped. "He was wearing a polo shirt and slacks when I showed him to Michael. So he was just a man with gray hair. And a beard, of course. I told Michael we had seen him a few weeks ago on the Early Show, only then he didn't have a beard, and Michael was very polite about it. He said, 'The one with the funny automobiles?' Which, as I recall, it was."

"They all are," Heimrich said. "Naturally enough."

"Actually," Susan said, "the men seem to stand up better than the women. It gives one pause. Accent on maturity."

And there she had gone again, harping on it. Damn the man. And there wasn't, really, anything to harp on. He wasn't ninety. He was a lot younger than Francis Dale, and look at Francis Dale. Drinking a Bloody Mary in a green velvet coat.

"La Belford?" she said, changing the subject slightly.

Peggy Belford had not been in the taproom of the Old Stone Inn of Van Brunt.

"They space it out," Heimrich said. "Seem to, anyway. To lessen the impact, naturally." He stopped. "I suppose," he said, in belated revision. Falling into speech habits is, of course (not "naturally") a sign of approaching senility. He must remember that, if he could.

"Of course," she said. "Two suns would dazzle the natives."

"And diminish each other," Heimrich said. "Na—"

She laughed then, softly, and in an instant, but for an instant only, they were close as sometimes (before the photograph) they had been close. He would take that damn hand out of that damn pocket and— Oh, the great *oaf!*

"They're all taking off in a few days," Heimrich said. "That's the word. Protective patrol to be recalled, which pleases them at the barracks. No longer a surging mob to be kept in check."

"Was there ever?"

There had been, as surging mobs go in western Putnam County, an area of tossed hills above a great river. But, for the first day only. After that there had been nothing much for state troopers to do. Heimrich chuckled suddenly. "Hear about the 'copter?" he asked

Susan and Susan moved her head slowly from side to side, and smiled slowly. He was coming out of it.

"They were making long shots of the house," Heimrich said. "And a bright red 'copter came down at roof level, making a 'copter's racket. Anton Zersk practically went up to join it, they tell me. From a standing start."

"The director?" Susan said and, when Heimrich nodded, that one could see how he might have felt like rocketing, going into orbit. "An old Dutch mansion in"—she considered briefly—"the late seventeenth, with a helicopter on its roof. Why didn't they just build it on a set? And—it isn't that old anyway. The Van Brunt mansion, I mean."

It was not; not by fifty years at least. And the rear of it was in a state of collapse.

"I don't know," Heimrich said. "Oh, I suppose 'filmed in the historic Hudson Valley, where the patroons'—the patroons what?"

"'Held sway,'" Susan said, without hesitation. "A talking point."

"Yes," Heimrich said. "And—nobody can fake the river. Give it that." They both looked down at the river. Nobody could fake the river.

"Dale and Miss Belford and a man named Latham were the only principals they brought along," Heimrich said. "And a lot of bit players. The rest are technicians and—God knows what. God and, I suppose, Marley. The producer."

He seemed, Susan said, to know a good deal about the visitors from—"from another planet." Which Hollywood might as well be.

Allied Pictures had sought the co-operation of the state police with somewhat elaborate thoroughness. News had reached Heimrich, who was professionally unconcerned, by osmosis. Since Van Brunt was the nearest community providing suitable accommodations, at least for Francis Dale and Peggy Belford, for Paul Marley and others of suitable rank, Heimrich had seen most of them around. Since Heimrich lived, when he could, at the Old Stone Inn.

She smiled again, gently, at that. Eighteen months ago—wasn't it?—a solid captain of the Bureau of Criminal Investigation of the New York State Police, had decided that the Old Stone Inn at Van Brunt would be a "convenient" place to live. Convenient to what? she might have asked, and had not, knowing. To a fabric shop across Van Brunt Avenue, to a hilltop house which once had been a barn. And—had slowed to a walk. The—*the bump on a log.* As if there were all the time in the world, which there never was.

Nor, she thought, is there now and said, "What time is it, dear?" (She could allow herself the "dear." That would not alarm him. She had heard that La Belford called everyone "darling." La Faye could be allowed a trifle.)

It was a little after six. Heimrich had to take his hand out of his pocket to look at his watch. For a moment she thought he might not put the hand back in the pocket. He did.

"He said anytime after six-thirty," she said. "When he telephoned this morning. The show at the library closed this afternoon, you know, and Brian had to collect his pictures, because next week is arts and crafts."

"God," Heimrich said.

"In which," Susan said, with formality, "I am showing two or three carefully chosen designs, representing modern examples of the still-continuing artistry of the Hudson Valley. Unquote."

"All right," Heimrich said. "I'm sorry."

He needn't be. His remark was appropriate. It represented an attitude which she fully shared. One, nevertheless, played along.

"Since large dogs have large appetites," she added. "To say nothing of small boys. We don't need to stay more than a few minutes. Brian said the thing just came to him, and, since it was so far out of his field, would I have a look at it? It's flattering, in a way. Since he's very good in his own line. You know?"

"Vaguely," Heimrich said. "Straight lines. A feeling that—that the air is very clear?"

He was not vague at all, she told him. It was precisely that quality which was the special value of Brian Collins's illustrations—his magazine covers, his commercial painting. She said Heimrich ought to be an art critic, since he had the, in that field, singular virtue of being comprehensible. She got, "Now Susan."

"Actually," she said. "It's what you've got, really. The critical mind. You see—oh, something that doesn't shape as it should. You say, 'Huh-uh.' You keep on looking until you see what is wrong with the—the picture, the situation."

Heimrich smiled at her. The smile changed his square face—re-formed it; in some fashion she had never understood, revealed it.

"Do I?" he said.

"Perhaps," she said, "a spur-of-the-moment notion. A way of saying it. I'll have to put a skirt on if you really mean the Bird and Bottle."

"I do," Heimrich said.

She stood up and he stood too. He was not quite a head taller. And—what *was* the matter with her—she had stood on the wrong side of the chaise, so that its breadth was between them. And in that instant she could tell by his eyes—oh, *damn*. Oh damn *and* damn. I deserve what I'm not getting, Susan Faye thought, and said that she wouldn't be a minute and went off across the terrace, a tall and slender young woman in white shorts and a soft white blouse who had, Heimrich thought, watching her lithe walking, got up on the far side of a wide chaise so that he wouldn't, great hulking hippo-potamus that he was, get any embarrassing notions. She was kind; she didn't want to hurt his feelings.

He knotted a tie in a white shirt. Which, he thought, was more than a hippopotamus could do. He could give himself that. She came back, a green wrap-around skirt smooth around slender hips, swinging about slim brown legs. She moved crisply, now.

There is a time to moon, Susan Faye had thought, buttoning a skirt of pale green linen around a slim waist, over white shorts. There is a time not to moon, she thought, running a comb through short brown hair. Mooning gets me nowhere, she decided, refreshing the color of a wide mouth, of softly curved lips which were getting damn tired of waiting. Not today. Not, at any rate, so far today. And why, knowing the bump on the log was moving far enough off it to reach a terrace, had she agreed to stop by Brian Collins's house, and studio, and tell him whether what he thought was a fabric design *was* a fabric design, or could be made into one? Or ought to be made into one.

Perhaps her asking the great oaf if he minded stopping by with her, if only for a minute, had been the throwing of the monkey wrench. The setting up of a time to do something else, hence the delimitation of their own time—possibly it was that which had, to-day, put him off. There would be no reason to it, but there did not have to be—not with Merton Heimrich. Or, admit it, with anybody worth the bother. These things are balanced on razor edge.

She walked out on the terrace, the sun on her. Heimrich was a big, solid man in sports jacket and gray slacks, in white shirt and a dark gray tie. A stolid man, she had thought—in a flicker of the most casual thought—when she had first seen him, after the fire house had burned down, before the charred body of Orville Phipps had turned up in its ashes. A man who, identified as a policeman, had fitted perfectly into preconceptions. No doubt a slow, sure man; a man who, called in to do a policeman's work, would inspire confidence if by no means promise brilliance.

He still looked much the same, except that now she did not see, at all clearly, what he looked like from the outside. And part of it had been right—he was unhurried, if not slow; he was thorough; he got what he started out to get. (Her out of a burning house, for example.) He was also, by and large, as intricate a person as any she had ever met. And as—as skittish.

She smiled faintly at her own choice of a word, moving toward—moving crisply toward, since this was no longer a time for mooning —an extremely solid man, who looked a little as if he had been planted on the terrace and was growing there, like an oak. Skittish indeed!

Seeing her smile, Heimrich thought of straightening his tie. He did not, being by no means a fidgeter. Well, if something about him amused her, it did not matter. There would be only friendliness in her amusement. He knew her well as a person; knew her to be without malice. (Or as closely as it was human to be.) She liked him. There was no doubt in his mind of that. She seemed to have affection for large animals.

Colonel sat part way up at her approach. He did not sit all the way up, preferring to be sure that the effort—in his case considerable —would be worth the trouble. "No, Colonel," Susan Faye said. "Not this time."

It was no more than Colonel had expected. Whatever he had done that was wrong was still held against him. They had taken the small god—the real god—away from him because he had done wrong, and still his expiation was incomplete. They would not let him go for a ride. Colonel thudded down on the flagstones again and sighed. "Poor Colonel," Susan said, and patted the great head. Colonel moaned at that.

"It's only," Susan Faye said, "because you're so outsized. Such a great lump of animal."

She doesn't, Captain M. L. Heimrich told himself sternly, mean any more than she said.

II

He DIDN'T, HEIMRICH said, know his way precisely. She would have
to guide. First along Oak Road?

"And then," Susan said, "left on Sugar Creek Lane until the end.
Or almost. Why Sugar Creek, do you suppose? There isn't any creek,
as far as I know."

It was to be supposed that once there had been; that somehow
sugar had been associated. Perhaps there had been sugar maples,
although this was not the region for them. Perhaps someone—fifty
years ago; three hundred years ago—had dropped a bag of sugar in a
tiny stream. Or the stream, come upon by thirsty men, had seemed,
after brackish water, of unexampled "sweetness." Possibly Brian Collins would know, since he lived at the end of the lane named for
the creek.

Susan doubted that. They were easy again, now; the tension was
gone now. They drove, climbing, toward the setting sun. It was
seven-fifteen, the car clock said. They talked of matters of no conceivable importance, and not to avoid discussing what had importance. It was a waiting time; a time between.

She doubted it because Brian Collins was, by the standards of the
countryside, a newcomer. She did not know him particularly well;
it was only since she had opened her shop on Van Brunt Avenue
that she had known him at all. He had dropped in one day—a year
ago? a year and a half ago?—and looked at fabrics, with the eye of a
man who sees color. He had introduced himself; had said that, in a
sense, he was in the same line of business. He had given his name.

"And I," Susan said, as the car turned into Sugar Creek Lane and
continued to climb, "said, like any other half-wit, 'The Brian Col-

lins?' And he asked what the hell anybody was supposed to say to a question like that, and why the hell did people keep on asking it, and if I meant did he do magazine covers and illustrations for nauseating stories, he supposed he was. He has moments of being abrupt, in a long-winded sort of way."

She had known vaguely for some time that Brian Collins lived in the area. She had thought it was nearer Cold Harbor, up the river a few miles. A good many people who lived on the back lanes in the town of Van Brunt went to Cold Harbor rather than to the Center to shop, partly because Cold Harbor had more places to shop in, and partly because it had a railroad station. She had mentioned Collins to somebody—she had now forgotten to whom—and been told about him. Or, more precisely, something about him. "He doesn't join in," Susan said, explaining that, and explaining it, to Heimrich, fully.

Collins had bought a few acres, "on the last high hill," above the river and built a house there. An entirely modern house, largely of glass; a house which was at the same time a dwelling and a studio. That had been about eight years ago.

"He was married then," Susan said. "I suppose he built the house for his wife, but apparently it didn't work. Anyway, there isn't any wife now—hasn't been for years. He's never said anything about her. As a matter of fact, I don't know him at all well. Went up once with some other people—people from New York—and looked at some of his things. Ran into him once someplace else—at the Kelseys' in Cold Harbor, as I remember it. And he stops by the shop now and then and looks at my things. Once he bought yardage enough for curtains and once he took me to lunch at the Inn. It was that time, I think, that he said he was having a go at fabric designing, for the fun of it. And that if anything came of it, he'd ask me to give an opinion."

"And," Heimrich said, "make an offer?"

She doubted it. For one thing, anything she—or anybody, for that matter—would be likely to pay for a design would be peanuts compared to what a man like Collins got for, say, a magazine cover. For the other thing—"All right," Susan said, "I've got my own style. It's what I've got to—it must be just around the next bend."

Heimrich drove slowly around the next bend, which was extremely sharp, and stopped the car abruptly since there road ended and so, apparently, did earth. Twenty feet more, and they would have rolled off into the sky. (Which would have been a violation of traffic regulation, because there was clearly a sign which said "Stop," as well it might.) Heimrich looked at Susan enquiringly.

"There," she said, and pointed. A few feet ahead a narrow driveway, almost a trail, went off to the right—went to the right and went up. "He likes privacy," Susan said, with no special inflection. Heimrich turned the car carefully into the driveway and started up it. "Of course," Susan said, "he has a four-wheel-drive one." Heimrich moved the gear selector to point at "L" and realized that, in the year or so he had driven this car, that had never been necessary. Even a "four-wheel-drive one" would, he thought, need to wear spikes for this in slippery weather.

Trees overhung the road, so that they climbed through a tunnel—a twisting tunnel. If they met anybody else coming down—well, somebody would have to back. The upbound car, presumably. Which would be—

They did not meet anyone; they made the last turn without meeting anyone. And ahead there was, abruptly, a clearing and a house—a sleek house as Susan had promised; a house largely of glass and redwood; a house on one long level. The car rolled onto a smooth expanse of gravel; a turnaround which seemed to be, at the same time, the front lawn of the house. Heimrich swept the car around until it faced the way they had come, its back to an open garage where a jeep and a Buick station wagon stood shoulder to shoulder.

They walked across gravel to flagstones and across flagstones to a frameless glass door. At least, Heimrich presumed it was the door, since it had a glass knob set into it. It was part of a glass wall under a wide, upward-pitched overhang. Sun in winter, shade in summer, Heimrich thought and looked into the room.

Brian Collins's desire for privacy stopped, evidently, with a hidden house. Once the house was found it was as un-private as—as, obviously, a goldfish tank. A fishtank was precisely what, standing at the glass door in the glass wall, one looked into. Thirty feet or so from the wall Heimrich and Susan Faye looked through, seeking signs of movement within, there was another wall, also of glass. And beyond it the sunlight, entering through yet another wall of glass—this one at right angles to the partition wall, and on their left as they looked into the house—flickered on water.

"Tricky," Susan said. "A swimming pool inside, but with sliding glass panels on the west so that it can, in a way, be moved outside. There doesn't seem to be anybody home. Of course, there's a lot more to the house. Probably he's in the studio and—" She did not finish. There was a glass button almost invisible in the glass wall. She pressed it. Faintly, from within the fishtank house, they could hear chimes.

There were chairs—low and modern chairs, various in shape—in the room on which the door would open, if somebody would come to open it. Several of the chairs were grouped around a free-standing fireplace, with a hood on it. Heimrich looked at the grouped chairs and at the same time Susan pressed the glass button again and the chimes sounded again. And Heimrich said, "Wait, Susan." He spoke in a level, somehow distant voice, as if he gave an order to someone he did not know.

She turned to look at him. But he moved away from her, down the glass wall of the house, still looking into the house. A dozen feet from her he stopped and leaned a little forward, toward the glass. He stood so for several seconds and then came back.

"Collins wears a beard?" he said and when, slowly, in a puzzled tone, she said, "Yes. A beard like—" and stopped, Heimrich said, "I'm afraid there's trouble," and pulled on the glass knob in the door. It resisted. He pushed. It did not resist.

"Better wait," he said, and went in, and she did not wait, but went in after him—went after him toward the grouped chairs. And then, seeing, she made a little, gasping sound and put both slim hands up to her face.

A man with a pointed beard which had been yellow, almost golden yellow, but now was matted red, sat in one of the chairs— slumped in the chair. His right arm dangled over the chair's low arm, the hand lax, open. Below the hand, on the tile floor, there was a stubby automatic pistol.

The wound in the man's right temple was a torn and blackened wound. A contact wound. And the story was told. Heimrich stood looking, not moving closer—not yet. Then he started to turn away and Susan said, in a voice unlike her voice—in a voice half whisper, riffled air—"*Look!*"

She pointed and he looked—looked at a slender foot, with painted nails. A foot only.

They went around the fireplace—the pedestal of a fireplace.

The dead girl wore a brief bathing suit, a golden yellow bathing suit. She had tawny hair of deeper gold and she lay on her back with one leg drawn up; lay relaxed, as if she rested, with arms flung out; rested gracefully, perhaps in conscious grace. And she had been shot just below the left breast, and there seemed to be very little blood. They would know better when they moved her.

She had been very beautiful until—Heimrich bent down and touched the skin of the extended, perfect leg. The skin was perceptibly cool to the touch. It was nothing to go by, nothing at all sure to go by. He bent lower and touched the tile floor. Perceptibly cool; cooler than the body. Which would have made a difference. But, at a guess, the girl had stopped being beautiful, in any sense that mattered at all, several hours earlier.

Which was, he thought, a little odd, and stood straight and continued to look down at the body of Peggy Belford, co-star with Francis Dale in *The Last Patroon*, being filmed on location.

"Did—" he said, without turning, and then realized that, seconds before, he had heard Susan's feet on the tiled floor. He turned sharply. She was standing on the other side of the room, near the door to the terrace. She had her back to him and her hands were over her face. He went to her quickly. She did not turn, did not move, until he put his hands gently on her shoulders. She leaned back against him, then, and he could feel her body shaking against his. He held her slender body against his sturdy one and waited until the shaking—it was as if she were having a chill—ended. Then her body moved as she drew air deep into her lungs.

"All right now," she said. "It's—he killed her? Then himself?"

"That's the way it looks," Heimrich said.

She turned. He let his hands fall from her shoulders. They were no longer needed. She faced him, looked up at him and her gray eyes were, he thought, strangely dark. Of course, the light came from behind her, which might be it.

"I didn't—" she said, and stopped and he saw the muscles move in her slender neck as she swallowed. "Didn't know it looked like—the way it does look."

"I know," he said. "Susan—don't you want to go sit in the car? Or —take the car back?"

"I'm all right," she said. "It's—it's like some hideous parody." He closed his eyes momentarily. "The—the gold-colored bathing suit," she said. "And—and Brian's beard. I never thought of it as gold-colored before and—and this awful place. Like a—tank."

Goldfish. Dead goldfish in a gigantic goldfish bowl. And death a grotesque, labored joke.

"Of course," Susan said, and her voice was different, almost an everyday voice—"the suit blended with her hair. That's all that means. And—she had been swimming?"

"I don't—" Heimrich said, and went back across the room and touched the golden bathing suit on the slender, curving body. It felt slightly damp. But he could not be sure; it would not be anything he would be able to swear to, if it came to swearing to things. He came back to Susan and said, "Probably," and then, "Do you know where he kept his telephone?"

She didn't. She supposed there would be one in his studio. "Through there," she said, and then, "Come on. I'll show you."

It would be better, Heimrich thought, if she got out of this tank-like house; away from the chill of death. Heimrich shook himself, mentally. The chill, now that he had got around to noticing it, prosaically of air conditioning. And a man and a woman dead, not goldfish.

"Wait a moment," he said, and left her where she was standing and went back to the bodies, this time to that of Brian Collins. Collins had died in gray slacks and a blue polo shirt; a short-sleeved polo shirt. Heimrich touched one muscled forearm. He went again to the girl's body, and again touched the slim brown leg. The girl's body was perceptibly cool. The man's was not. Which would mean, other things being equal, that she had died before the man. But— other things are seldom equal. She had lain, almost naked, on a cool tile floor. He had sat in a chair, with most of his body clothed.

And, suppose Brian Collins had killed Peggy Belford—Peggy the beautiful; La Belford the exquisite—for reasons unknown and then, for reasons not too difficult to guess, himself. Suppose that and it was still not necessary to suppose the two actions had been as nearly as possible simultaneous in time. It is easier to kill another than one's self. Men have been known to need three shots for self-destruction, so anxiously does the body flinch away. They have been known to take hours steeling themselves for the attempt.

Anyway, a doctor could tell him more. It was high time to get a doctor on the way—a doctor and the rest. He turned to Susan and she came to him, but did not look at the bodies. She led him to a door in the wall beyond the fireplace—a quite conventional plastered wall —and said, "I think it's this way," and they went into a hall. At the end of the hall there was the open doorway to a kitchen. At right angles, leading toward the rear of the house, was another corridor, wood paneled. "Sliding doors," Susan said. "All the doors slide."

The house, Heimrich realized, was built like an L, a fact which was not apparent when one approached it from the front. This corridor ran along the foot of the L. It ended in a studio, with slanting skylight. There was an easel, draped with canvas; framed pictures were stacked against walls, their faces to the walls. And, leaning against a desk, there were half a dozen canvases, framed, tied into a bundle.

There was a telephone on the desk. Captain Heimrich used the telephone, a switch to start a machine.

"Look," Susan said, when he had finished, and he looked. She had lifted the shrouding cover from the picture on the easel.

The girl in the painting was not wearing a golden bathing suit. She was not wearing anything at all. She lay—as, in the other room, the dead girl lay—on her back on a green tile floor, with one perfect leg bent at the knee and lifted; with the head back on the floor and tawny-colored hair swirling about it. The face was turned a little toward the painter. It was a lovely face.

"There isn't any doubt, is there?" Susan Faye said, and Heimrich shook his head slowly. There wasn't any doubt. This very beautiful naked girl, delineated with exquisite attention to detail, was beyond question Peggy Belford.

"My guess would be," Susan Faye said, "that it was painted several years ago. And—Brian Collins loved beauty. Why would he kill anything so beautiful?"

The question could be assumed to be rhetorical. It could not, in any case, be answered. The statement—

"Why several years ago?" Heimrich asked.

"Because—" she said, and broke off. "I'm not an expert," she said. "It's only an impression. If it's important—"

Heimrich lifted his shoulders a little.

"An expert might be able to tell," she said. "But—how long have they been here? The movie people?"

They had been around for about two weeks.

"Pigments fade," she said. "It's—oh, there's a patina. Easier to see than to explain. I'm fairly sure that this wasn't painted within two weeks. I'd doubt if it was painted within two years."

"Fairly?" Heimrich said.

"All right," she said. "More than that. But, I'm not an expert, Merton."

"He never said anything about her?" Heimrich asked. "About knowing her."

This time she shrugged, quickly, almost impatiently. She had told him that she barely knew Brian Collins. She had no idea whom he might have known, might not have known. He had never mentioned knowing Peggy Belford. "But," she said, "I doubt if he would. Because—oh, because she *was* so well known. People would have said, 'You mean you *really* know her? Tell me—' It would have been like saying '*the*' Brian Collins."

It was not too clear; it was clear enough.

"Only," Heimrich said, "with them here—with the subject brought up. Almost anyone might have said—'Oh, I knew her once. She posed for me once, as a matter of fact.'"

"Until he called me this morning," Susan said. "Asked if I wanted to look at a design, I hadn't spoken to him in—months. So—I've no idea what he may have said since the subject was 'brought up.' And —you're being very like a policeman, aren't you?"

He smiled at that, and again the smile re-formed, revealed, his face.

"Now Susan," he said. "I *am* a policeman. There's no getting around it, naturally. You thought you'd find a fabric design on the easel?"

She had. It was because she had that she had lifted the drop sheet which covered the picture on the easel. It would have been the natural place for Collins to place his design for her to look at. The most obvious place. Clearly, he had not chosen the obvious place. It didn't matter now.

"No," Heimrich said. "Still—he did expect you. Unless, of course, something—the thing between him and Miss Belford—put it out of his mind. Still— You'd know this design if you saw it? I mean, he gave you some idea about it?"

She smiled faintly at that, smiled inwardly. You didn't tell people about designs when you could show them designs. She shook her head. "But," she said, "I'd know it was a fabric design. Not—" She looked at the picture on the easel. "Not a portrait. But—it doesn't matter now, does it?"

He said, again, that it didn't matter now. And, again, he said, "Still—" and looked around the studio; looked at the canvases on their stretchers, leaning against one another along the walls. He turned one so that it faced them. It was characteristic—rooftops in very clear air. He tried another.

"It won't be on canvas," Susan said. "On paper. Rolled up or, maybe, thumbtacked to a drawing board. About—oh—" She measured in the air; measured what seemed to be more or less a square, the sides four feet or a little more in length.

Heimrich abandoned the canvases. He moved along the wall, looking for a drawing board with paper thumbtacked to it.

"The point is," he said, "Collins expected you. Unless— Susan, you're sure it *was* Collins who called you? Asked you to stop by, look at the design?"

"Of—" she began, with confidence. But she stopped with that. "A man called," she said. "Said he was Brian Collins. You mean, am I sure from the voice? No. Except that there wasn't anything *wrong* with the voice. Nothing unexpected. You think it was somebody else? But—why? And, he called hours before—before this could have happened." She considered, was careful. "Somebody called," she said.

Heimrich said, "Hm-mm," and then, "This?"

He turned to face a drawing board with heavy paper taped—not thumbtacked—to it. He held it up. The paper was covered with colored blotches, irregular in form. Yet it was not haphazard.

"Yes," she said, and moved a little way, and back, and a little to one side, and back. "That could be it. Or one of them, if he did several." Heimrich, acting as easel, waited. "You can see what he was after," Susan said. "But—busy." She said this, Heimrich thought, more or less to herself. "And—" she said. "But it doesn't matter now. All that matters is that we've found it. So—it wasn't somebody else to—to get me here. And why would anybody?"

Heimrich had not, he said, the least idea. A question came up, even a very minor question. You answered it if you could. Answered it as you went along, if you could.

A plodder's way, Heimrich thought, leaning the board back where he had found it. And—his way. Which couldn't be helped. And there was certainly no point in telling Susan that he, clod that he no doubt was, considered Brian Collins's fabric design—well the word seemed to be "alarming." He could not see, even remotely, what Brian Collins had been "after." He tried to imagine the design,

[29]

printed on cloth, as the cover of, for example, a sofa. He abandoned the effort. Probably it was the sort of thing that anyone with imagination, anyone with a sense of color, would find admirable. Even exciting. Susan had certainly looked at it; for a moment, he thought, she had forgotten other things—even this evening's other things—while she looked. A thing—a perception—he didn't have. So—

Heimrich went over and stood in front of the painting of Peggy Belford. It, at any rate, spoke for itself; made no demands he could not meet.

"She was beautiful, wasn't she?" Susan said.

Heimrich nodded.

"Do you know," he said, "whether he did much of this sort of thing? Most of the things of his I remember were—oh, the edges of roofs; streets—villages. This is—what, Susan?"

"Calendar," she said. "Oh, superior calendar, I think. But—his style, if you're thinking somebody else did it. Also, it's signed." She pointed. The canvas was signed in the lower right-hand corner: "B. Collins," in the just decipherable blur of a painter's signature.

"The point is," Susan Faye said, "why is it here? Instead of the design? Set up to—to be looked at. By whom?"

"Yes," Heimrich said. "That is a point, Susan. Why, then?"

"For her to look at? She came—why?"

Heimrich shook his head. She had come; she had died. He waited.

"They talked about the past. There—there must have been a past?"

If she was right about the age of the picture, there must have been a past. The past, at least, of a painter and a model. A not remote past, clearly; Peggy Belford had died a young woman. They would have to find out how young; they would have to find out a good many things. She was certainly not a child when Collins had painted her.

"I'll say not," Susan Faye said.

Heimrich smiled at that, mildly. He said he saw her point. He said, "Go on, Susan. They were talking about the past?"

It was, she said, obvious enough. They had—it was impossible to guess what they had said, because it was impossible to guess at the tone of their exchange. Was it building then, already, toward—"toward that?" Susan said and moved her hand and arm a little, indicating what lay outside the studio. At any rate, they must have at some time said "remember?" of the painting, and set it up and looked at it.

"And—" Susan said, and stopped, and then said that that was as far as she could go. She waited. Heimrich closed his eyes. He nodded his head slowly, but his eyes were closed. Then he opened them.

They were guessing, Heimrich said. Hers was a good guess, probably. There was another.

"You knew him," he said, and, when she began to shake her head, "I know. Not well. But I didn't know him at all. Suppose—"

Suppose Collins had killed—in fury, perhaps. In outrage at something done, something said. And, seen her lying, not beautiful any more, on the floor of the living room. And—

"You say he loved beauty," Heimrich said. "He might have—in a sense have gone back to find her beauty, which he had destroyed. Got this out and stood looking at it—looking at what he had destroyed. For a long time perhaps, remembering whatever he had to remember. Then—then he went back."

Heimrich stopped for a moment, stood looking at the painting.

"You see, Susan," he said, "he—I suppose it was he—rearranged the body so that it was in the pose of this. Perhaps in some tormented effort to undo what he had done. Or, restore what he had destroyed. Because, people don't fall down gracefully when a thirty-eight slug hits them. They sprawl, my dear. It's a very ugly thing, Susan. He may have tried—well, to take some of the ugliness out. As a kind of final apology. Before he shot himself."

[31]

She looked at him; he could still surprise her.

"You're sure?" she said. "Not of all of it—the reasons. But, that her body was—posed?"

"Now Susan," Captain Heimrich said, "not sure, naturally. But, I think the odds are very high. Yes. The drawn-up knee. It's hard to see how it would have been just that way. And in the picture, the same position. Not sure. But—I'd say several hundred to one."

She said nothing for some seconds. Then she said, "May I cover it again?" and when he said, "Of course, dear," lifted the cover canvas and let it fall over the picture.

"The curtain coming down," she said. "That's what— That's it! It's all—unreal. Composed. As if—" She stopped, and looked at him through widened gray eyes. "As if, out there, too, the curtain might go down and they would get up and—and *take bows*."

"Yes," Heimrich said.

"It's uglier," she said. "Not—not better. As if it were all some—" She did not finish, and he could see that she had begun again to tremble. He put his arms around her and she trembled in his arms, and then grew quiet, then freed herself.

"I'm sorry," she said. "I'm a hindrance, really. I'm sorry, dear."

"No," Heimrich said. "You said—composition. Or, rather, composed. As a painter thinks of composition?"

She supposed so.

"It seems to me," Heimrich said, "rather more like a scene. From a play. You said that too, of course. The dead fall gracefully, in acceptable patterns. A matter of direction."

Her eyes widened again.

"I don't know, Susan," Heimrich said. "I'll have to try to find out."

Faintly, they heard the sound of a siren. That would be a cruise car, Heimrich thought. A cruise car would almost certainly be first.

III

It would, Sergeant Charles Forniss said, be a matter of going through the motions. Because, Forniss said, there wasn't really anything wrong with the way it looked. "Of course," he said, "it'll be interesting if he turns out to have been left-handed."

"Or," Heimrich said, "if there was a dog that didn't bark."

To this Forniss, driving the police car carefully down the steep drive from the sleek house on the hilltop, said, "Huh?" and was told not to worry about it.

"A literary reference," Heimrich said. "Not apropos. It won't turn out he was left-handed. And, as you say, there isn't really anything wrong with the way it looks. Including the time element."

What was to be done at the house was, for Heimrich and Forniss, done. Others remained; the collectors remained—the men who sought dust in an almost dustless house, and fibre fragments and things in desks which might prove helpful. (A signed statement, saying, "I killed Peggy Belford and am now going to shoot myself," would be among the latter. It was not expected.) The photographers had taken pictures of the bodies from many directions; a sketch artist had looked at the living room and sighed and done a detail sketch of it. Then the bodies had been taken away. All the motions were being gone through, and probably it was a great waste of time.

The house had been measured, fore and aft, its dimensions set forth in lines and figures. ("I now show you a floor plan of the house of the late Brian Collins and ask you—") It had been discovered and noted down that the glass panels between living room and pool responded to manual pressure but that the similar panels between pool and terrace were operated electrically. And could be so operated either from the pool room or from the terrace. The plan showed the bedrooms off the corridor which ran back to the studio, and the kitchen at the start of the same corridor, and the shower stall and dressing room accessible both from the pool, at its far end, and the studio. (Convenient both for swimmers and, presumably, for models Collins might have used.)

All the motions had been, or were being, gone through. The routine is fixed, nothing escapes it. And it was highly probable that, in this case, routine wasted much time and no little energy.

"It won't be the first time a guy's killed a dame and waited two-three hours to finish the job," Forniss said, and went carefully down and around a steep corner on Sugar Creek Lane. "On himself," Forniss added.

That there had been at least that period of time between the deaths of Peggy Belford and Brian Collins had been partially, if somewhat grudgingly, confirmed by the physician, representing the Putnam County coroner's office, who had examined the bodies. People were all the time expecting the impossible, asking for definite answers when only guesses were available; refusing to wait for the results of autopsies. But, if Heimrich had to have it—the woman had died sometime between two and four, and the median time was the best guess; the man was alive then, and at least until five and was certainly dead by six-thirty.

"Because," Forniss said, "killing somebody else is one thing and killing yourself is another. And getting that picture out and maybe spending an hour or so looking at it. People like that do crazy things. Artists."

"All kinds of people do crazy things, Charlie," Heimrich said.

"Not," Forniss said, "that she wasn't something to look at. Alive. You really figure he fixed the body up to look like the picture?"

"Somebody did," Heimrich said. "I suppose he did. At least, I never saw anybody lie like that after a thirty-eight slug caught them. Did you, Charlie?"

"Nope," Forniss said. "And, when they check the bullets, they'll be from the same thirty-eight."

"Turn right down here," Heimrich said. "I'll stop by Mrs. Faye's and pick up the car. Yes, I don't doubt they will be. If it isn't the way it looks, nobody is going to have made it that easy."

The bullet which had killed the man had gone through his head, the wound of entrance torn and gaping, that of exit small and neat, and lodged in a chair, from which it had been extracted. The bullet had been battered as it battered bone. It was where they had first looked, assuming that Collins had held the automatic against the side of his head and pulled the trigger as he sat in the chair they had found him in. The ejected shell had rolled on the tile floor, but was near enough the expected place.

The bullet which had killed the woman had been fired from not less than four feet away and, probably, not more than ten. She probably had been standing at the time and the course of the bullet through her body was slightly upward—an autopsy would confirm the physician's immediate judgment, the physician was reasonably certain. So Collins might well have been sitting in a chair and she standing in front of him. The bullet had gone through the heart and Peggy Belford had been dead in that instant. Hence, the small quantity of blood. Cadavers do not bleed. Collins had lived at least for some minutes, as those with brain injuries often do.

The bullet which had killed the woman had been found partly embedded in wall paneling, again in an area which had appeared most probable, assuming she had been shot near where she lay dead. This bullet was little damaged.

There were other things; other bits and pieces, at the moment proving nothing. The girl had been in the pool, almost certainly. When her body had been photographed, could be moved, it was found that the back of the fragmentary bathing suit was perceptibly damp. They had found a white beach coat on a chair at the far end of the pool. Presumably it was hers; presumably she had worn it, over the golden bathing suit, when she came to Collins's house. Presumably she had come in the station wagon. Presumptions were everywhere. They could guess and guess again.

On a clothesline in the rear of the house they had found a pair of swimming trunks, black, damp. The day was humid; the trunks, when they were found, had been hanging in the shade. Collins's, presumably; worn that day, almost certainly. Had they been in the pool together, or at different times? There was nothing to indicate.

There were smudges on the butt of the .38 automatic, and more smudges on the barrel. Nothing that told them anything, or ever would. There was a partial print, apparently Collins's, on the base of one of the ejected shells. So, presumably he had put the shells in the clip. Which was nothing of a surprise, nor proof of anything. The gun was his. He had a permit for it; the permit was in his neatly ordered desk.

Bits and pieces, odds and ends. Items to be noted down; notes to be filed. They went through the motions; added totals, knowing the answers. A successful commercial artist in his late thirties had shot and killed an extremely beautiful motion picture actress and then, after a rather long pause, shot and killed himself.

Neither Heimrich nor Forniss said anything for some minutes. The police car moved slowly down hill, around curves, generally toward the east, generally toward Van Brunt Center.

"So," Sergeant Forniss said, "why don't you buy it?"

"Now Charlie," Heimrich said. "What makes you think I don't?"

"Come off it," Charles Forniss said, friend to friend, not sergeant to captain.

"No," Heimrich said. "I think probably I'll have to buy it. As you say, there's nothing wrong with it. A little arranged, maybe. A little—"

He did not finish immediately. Forniss edged the police car to the side of Sugar Creek Lane and a small, eager car went past it, driven by a young, eager man.

"Teddy Barnes," Forniss said. "Deadline Wednesday night and here it is Saturday already."

Theodore Barnes was managing editor—with two reporters to manage—of the Cold Harbor *Weekly Chronicle*, published every Thursday of the year.

"Now Charlie," Heimrich said. "He'll cover for the New York papers. Until they can get their own men here. It's going to make a stir, you know."

"And how," Forniss said, and turned right off Sugar Creek Lane into Oak Road. "If you don't buy it as it stands, they'll love you. You know that?"

"Yes," Heimrich said. "So—we buy it, Charlie."

"For now," Forniss said.

"For now," Heimrich repeated.

Forniss turned left into High Road and slowed and looked enquiringly at Heimrich.

"Drop me at the drive," Heimrich said. "You may as well start with Collins. I'll pick you up at the Inn sometime around—" He looked at his watch. It was almost nine o'clock. "Around ten-thirty," he said. "Get something to eat, Charlie."

Forniss asked if Heimrich had never known him not to and watched the captain walk up the driveway, between two ill-placed boulders. (A car coming out of that drive had to come out by inches or risk the loss of its ears.) A nice girl Heimrich had found. Forniss wished him luck and drove on toward the Center.

She had been watching for him. She stood on the edge of the terrace and looked at him gravely. When he came up to her she held out both hands, and he took both her hands. He said he was sorry as hell, but that was the way things were. She said, "You're going to have a drink. *And* something to eat. Lamb curry, which won't take five minutes. And—it was the way it looked?"

"It—" he began, but she said, "Wait a minute. The drink first. It runs to variety nowadays. Gin or bourbon."

They sat with martinis, not on the chaise; in terrace chairs on either side of a terrace table.

"We haven't found anything to change it," Heimrich said. "Murder and suicide. Only—she was his wife, Susan."

She said, inelegantly, with her eyes widening, "Huh?"

"Had been," Heimrich said. "Perhaps a better way to put it, he was one of her husbands. The first, apparently. I'd guess she was the wife he built the house for."

Susan said, reflectively, that she'd be damned.

"One of the boys," Heimrich said, "one of the troopers, is a fan. Reads movie magazines. Only—it wasn't any secret, Susan. Apparently everybody knows about it."

"Everybody," Susan said, "whose interests therein lie. Not, for one, me."

He sipped martini, which was cold and almost innocent of vermouth. He said she could make it two. He said that the trouble with them was that they didn't keep up with things.

"With Hollywood marriages?" she said. "Does anyone? Including those involved?"

It appeared that many did. Perfect marriages flowered amid cheers, withered to the accompaniment of universal sobs. It was another world. She agreed. She looked into the cocktail pitcher. She said, "This is ice water. Wait." She went and returned. She poured and said, "Go on, Ricky."

He choked over his first sip. He looked at her wildly.

"When I got back with your car," she said, "I hadn't anything in particular to think about that—well, that I wanted to think about. If you know what I mean? Up there wasn't—" She shivered, in spite of the warmth of the July evening.

"So," she said, "I thought. He hates Merton. For no reason, but that's his business. So, what? And I thought, there's a man at the club named Robinson, but everybody calls him Robby. Including his wife. So—"

She paused and looked at him. His blue eyes were very wide open.

"So," she said, "I decided on Ricky. Unless you mind?"

"Including—" Heimrich said, as if from a great distance, and she waited, leaning a little forward. "I don't mind at all," he said. "I— I don't mind at all." He paused for a longer time, and she waited, did not prompt, did not say, "Including, you were going to say?"

"Naturally," Heimrich said.

She sighed, inaudibly. "About Peggy Belford?"

"Oh," Heimrich said. "I'm having it checked out in New York. My trooper doesn't remember what happened back in the dim ages— eight years ago or so, apparently. He thinks she was a dancer or singer in New York, and that Collins married her there. Lasted about two years, he thinks and then, probably, she got a Hollywood offer. She married two-three times after that. My boy thinks her last marriage ended about a year ago. It was to a man named Roland something."

"Brian was trying to get her to come back?"

"Now Susan," Heimrich said. "How would I know that?"

"It could have been that. Only—"

He waited.

"Ricky," she said, a little tentatively. He did not object. He did not even close his eyes. "Ricky," she said, "I don't believe it. It's— it's wrong."

There was only one question for that, and Heimrich asked it.

"It's no good saying he wasn't the type, is it?" Susan said. "Because you'll say, 'Who is?' Or, equally, 'Who isn't?'"

"Now Susan," Heimrich said. "No. I like to see the character fit the crime. Why wasn't he?"

"Too—sure," she said. "Of himself. I said he might have been trying to get her to come back. Implying that, when she wouldn't, he got into a—a jealous rage, I suppose. And killed her. Only, that was just something to say. Something that leaped to the mind."

"Because," Heimrich said, "it's obviously the way—a way—it looked."

"All right," she said. "I only met him a few times. I told you that. It isn't enough to go on, and I realize that."

"Go anyway."

"A man who would do that would be—what? Not sure of himself, wouldn't he? Emotionally unstable, to use a cliché for it. Not sufficient, of himself. So that, with something he wanted taken away from him, he'd go into a tantrum. Like a child. Say, 'You give me what I want or else.' Well—I don't believe it. If a woman walked out on Brian Collins he'd—all right, he'd have been likely to think the loss was hers and the hell with it. I'm not very coherent, am I?"

"Enough," Heimrich said.

"And you think I'm basing a lot on a few meetings. With other people, mostly. Once, as I told you, at lunch. Probably I am."

"My dear," Heimrich said, "you're an intelligent woman. Observant. Meeting a person a few times you'd get an over-all impression. Call it an outline of the person. Unless there was a deliberate effort to mislead—"

"No," she said. "He wouldn't go to the trouble. Wait—that's what I'm trying to say. He wouldn't have gone to *this* trouble. He'd say, 'Take it or leave it. Take *me* or leave me.'"

She had grown more eager as she sought words for the intangible. And now, suddenly, what she had herself said seemed to deflate her.

"Except," she said, "that he obviously did go to the trouble. So I'm wrong. So I'll go put the curry on to heat."

She went, and he watched her with pleasure. He finished his drink and picked up the glasses and followed her. They would, of course, have to find other people who had known Brian Collins—known him longer. But whatever they learned would be nothing to take to a jury, if anybody was ever brought before a jury, which seemed arrestingly improbable. (What was Brian Collins's reputation in the community in which he lived? That of a man who would not kill himself. So? Was all physical evidence consonant with the theory that Brian Collins shot and killed Peggy Belford, once his wife, and then himself? Yes. So?)

"Let it lie, captain," the district attorney would say. "Let it lie, for God's sake. Your girl friend says he wasn't the type. Let it lie, captain."

And what have I got against its being the way it looks? Heimrich asked himself, carrying glasses into the small kitchen off the enormous living room. "In a minute," Susan said, stirring. "Take Colonel with you."

Colonel was morosely occupying most of the kitchen, looking fixedly at what Susan stirred. Heimrich told him to come on, and he looked at Heimrich, and Heimrich said, sternly, "Come on," and went back into the living room. To the surprise of everybody, Colonel went with him.

Except, Heimrich thought, continuing his self-investigation, that it's somehow too damned elaborate. Too made up. He went back to the kitchen door. "Was Collins's composition good?" he asked Susan, who said, "Very," without looking around.

The curry was excellent; coffee after it was admirable. Heimrich sighed slightly, and said he was sorry about the evening and that he would have to get on with it. She walked with him to the door.

It was dusk, now. They stood close. "Well," Merton Heimrich said, slowly. "I'll have—"

He stopped. Car lights advanced up the steep drive. (Damn, Susan Faye thought.) A tall young man who wore glasses got out of a light panel truck. He came up onto the terrace and said, "Captain Heimrich?" and, when Heimrich nodded, "Fine. They said I might find you here." He looked at Susan. "With Mrs. Faye," he said. "Name's Alder."

Heimrich said, "Good evening, Mr. Alder."

"Burt Alder," the tall young man—the quite young man—said. "Press representative with the unit."

"Oh," Heimrich said. "Sergeant Forniss will give you what we've got."

"Nope," Alder said. "Not a reporter. Was once but there's no money in it. O.K., make it press agent. Allied Pictures. Came along with the unit. Never tell when there might be an item. But this— God. They're sending Framingham east on this. Company plane."

Heimrich raised his eyebrows.

"Head of the publicity department," Alder said. "Me, the boy who holds his thumb in the dike. Or was it a finger?"

"Dike?"

"Manner of speaking, captain. They're going to make a thing out of this, if we aren't careful. What I'm after is co-operation. Bad enough without making it any worse, don't you see?"

"I'm afraid," Heimrich said, "that I don't get what you're talking about, Mr. Alder. Who's going to make a thing out of— I suppose you mean out of Miss Belford's death? Mr. Collins's?"

"I tell you," Alder said, "the Inn's swarming with reporters. And it's going to get worse. M. G.'s not going to like it, captain."

"I'm sorry," Heimrich said. "It's nothing anybody likes particularly. Who, or what, is M. G.?"

Burt Alder looked at Heimrich with utter astonishment.

"M. G. Drisken," he said, making it most distinct. And Heimrich shook his head.

"My God," Alder said. "That's all I can say."

"Suppose," Heimrich said, "we sit down over here, Mr. Alder, and you tell me whatever it is you've come up here to tell. Starting, at the moment, with the man you call 'M. G.'"

"*The* M. G. Drisken," Alder said, in a final effort. He spoke as a man underneath whose feet the ground had shaken. He looked anxiously at Susan Faye.

"Wait," Susan said. "I think he's something in the movies."

"*Something,*" Alder said. "Oh my—" He did not finish. He regained control. "Mr. Drisken," he said, formally—rather as if Mr. Drisken were present, listening—"is head of Allied Pictures. You've heard of Goldwyn? Of—Zanuck?" He looked at Heimrich. Heimrich nodded. "Drisken," Alder said. "He won't like this, as I said. We've got to handle it. Minimize the damage." He walked over to a chair and sat in it. Heimrich went to another, but Susan hesitated. Heimrich made a summoning motion with his head. "I may," he said, "need an interpreter."

"I'm sorry," Alder said. "The point is, we're—well, we're—well, say we're all shook up. Marley particularly. It was he said, 'Boy, you'd better get right out there. Arrange for co-operation.'" He paused, having learned his lesson. "Paul Marley," he said. "He's the producer. The man who—"

"I know what a producer is," Heimrich said. "Co-operation as to what, Mr. Alder?"

"Captain," Alder said, "they've got two in the cans. Starring—anyway, featuring—Belford. One's going to be released next month and— All right. Listen. In it she's this pure librarian type. Wears glasses, for God's sake. Got no idea she's beautiful, see? Demure. That's the word. All the guys see her in it think, first, what a damned sweet little thing she is but, at the same time, that she's a dish.

Like maybe the girl next door. Only a dish. And so she gets killed in an artist's studio—an *artist's*, for the love of God. Without a stitch on."

"No," Heimrich said, "she was wearing a bathing suit, Mr. Alder. If that helps."

"It's something," Alder said. "Not a lot."

"No," Heimrich said, "it wasn't a lot."

"Some of the babes," Alder said, "it wouldn't matter. Some of them—hell, you build them up that way. They get married a lot, or they go around a lot with somebody, but they're stacked—that's what you want. They get killed in a lover's quarrel, so what? I mean, that is, that it won't hurt box office. For what's already canned, of course."

"Of course," Heimrich said.

"Babes like Belford," Alder said, "you have their pictures taken wearing aprons. With a kid or two, if possible."

"Did Miss Belford have any children?" Susan asked, and was looked at in honest astonishment.

"That babe?" Alder said. "And risk that shape? It's the *idea* I'm talking about."

"Mr. Alder," Heimrich said, "I've got quite a lot of things to do. What is it you want? To have us report that Miss Belford was wearing a tweed suit? And—spectacles?"

"It's nothing to joke about," Alder said. "There's a hell of a lot of money involved. And, listen—in this one they're shooting now. She's a milkmaid. Give you my word. An honest to God *milkmaid*. And this Dutch patroon, who owns half the Hudson River, meets her and she doesn't realize how beautiful she is or what he's up to, really, and she's as innocent as—" He stopped for a simile, waited, gave it up. "You're sure she was wearing a bathing suit?" he asked, clinging to that. "Down in the village the story is—"

"She was," Heimrich told him. "What'll they do now about the picture? The one they're making?"

There, Burt Alder said, they had a break. They'd shot all the scenes Peggy Belford was important in. Finished with them the day before. There were still a couple of long shots, but for them they could use a stand-in.

"One of them is with cows," Alder said. "She'll have had to have a stand-in for that one anyway. Scared to death of cows, La Belford was. Men, no. Cows, yes. What you'd call irony, come to think of it."

They allowed a brief pause to commemorate the irony of it all.

"You've probably got out biographical material about her," Heimrich said. "Your office has, anyway. Mentioning she had once been married to Collins?"

"In passing," Alder said. "You want a fill-in? We co-operate. You co-operate."

"Start with you," Heimrich said. "A brief fill-in, yes."

"The way it was? Or the way we prettied it?"

Heimrich sighed. He said, "Just an outline, Mr. Alder."

In outline: Peggy Belford—"her real name, far's I know"—had been in a chorus line at a night club eight years ago. In New York. And Collins, who lived in New York then, met her and used her as a model and married her. "The way we had it," Alder said, "they met because she was interested in art. Sort of a suggestion, without pinning it down, that she was studying art. Aspiring young artist. See what I mean?"

"She wasn't?"

"Hell. How do I know? Aspiring, sure as hell. I mean—" They waited. "Never mind. So, she gets a screen test in a couple of years and a contract, and goes to Hollywood and he doesn't. So it's Las Vegas, or maybe Reno, and then Ricky Monterray. The band leader."

"Ricky?" Susan Faye repeated, in a distant voice.

"Why not?" Alder said. "He marries damn near everybody, sooner or later. So she gets a part as a pure little salesgirl in a dress shop, demure as hell."

"Wearing glasses?" Susan asked, with interest.

Alder looked at her, with some uncertainty. She did not amplify.

"Probably," he said. "Anyhow, there was something about an evening dress to be modeled and the model broke her leg or something and our Peggy steps into the dress, which is the kind of dress a dame sticks out of and—O.K. There you are. The start of a career."

"The perpetual Cinderella," Susan said.

"All right," Alder said. "Show me a better story. House dress to sables, and all on the up and up. The men drool over Belford and the girls drool over what she wears."

"And take their own glasses off," Susan said. "And go around bumping into things."

Alder laughed at that, and said she had it.

"After this Ricky," Heimrich said, and paused and did not look at Susan. "After this Mr. Monterray? I gather she didn't stop there. Stay there?"

"You don't keep up with things," Alder said.

"No," Heimrich said. "Probably not. After Monterray?"

"For the record," Alder said. "For our record, he left her and she was brokenhearted and what have you. Poor trusting little thing, abandoned by a wolf. You keep the image."

"Now Mr. Alder," Heimrich said. "Keep it, by all means. But, in fact?"

"Hell," Alder said. "They both played around. Who doesn't?" He was not answered, since an answer might have taken time. "So—phfft, as somebody used to say. Then—the big league. Francis Dale, no less."

Heimrich closed his eyes briefly. He opened them and repeated the name.

"Why not?" Alder said. "She was a dish. Frank likes dishes. In a quiet, marrying way, you understand."

Heimrich said he understood. He said he would gather that this marriage had been—what? A step up?

He could call it that.

"And," Susan said, "she slipped off it? Or, stepped off it?"

"Well," Alder said, "Dale's a good deal older. Anyway, it lasted a couple of years and they rifted."

"Which must," Susan said, "have presented a problem." Alder looked at her enquiringly in the dim light.

"Not too much of a problem. Incompatibility. Everybody can have one incompatibility," he said. "So then a man named Fielding. Roland Fielding. Not in the profession, so it didn't matter. Nobody's ever heard of him. Automobile dealer, or something like that."

"Until?"

"About a year ago. Extreme cruelty. But no publicity to speak of. Nobody gave a damn. Which brings us back to this."

"Which is a problem?" Heimrich said.

"Two pictures on the shelf," Alder said. "Not counting *The Last Patroon*. What do you think of that as a title, by the way? We're sort of making a survey."

"I think," Susan said gravely, "that it lacks something."

"What I keep telling them," Alder said. "What's a patroon? they'll want to know, and figure it's a misprint. Anyway. Our demure milkmaid and what have you gets herself killed in an artist's studio and so she's obviously no better than she should be and so what do we get? Pressure groups. So—"

He looked at Heimrich intently.

"I don't," Heimrich said, "see what can be done about it. Actually, of course, Miss Belford was merely having a swim in a pool owned by a former husband, and was wearing as much as attractive girls normally do under such circumstances."

"You don't get it," Alder said. "Listen—the man was an artist. He did paintings."

Heimrich said he was sorry. He stood up.

"Listen," Alder said. "You got me off the track. Why couldn't it have been an accident? Say he was cleaning his gun, maybe. She'd dropped in for tea, because she and her former husband were on the friendliest of terms and she was in the neighborhood anyway. And he was cleaning his gun and—" Alder stopped.

"You see the difficulties," Heimrich said. "He's cleaning his gun, while he's serving tea. It goes off by accident and kills Miss Belford. And then—what? He cleans it again and it goes off by accident and kills him?"

"Well—"

"Mr. Alder, did you really expect what you call 'co-operation?' A hush-up of some sort?"

"If you mean me," Alder said, and stood up too. "No, I guess not. Not that that sort of thing hasn't happened."

"Not here," Heimrich said. "Not that I ever heard of."

"All right," Alder said. "Marley said make a pitch and I made a pitch. I'll pass the word."

"This Mr. Framingham," Heimrich said. "He may as well stay in Hollywood. Hold M. G.'s hand."

"Don't," Alder said, "expect me to tell him that, captain." He started off. He stopped. "Somebody said," Alder said, "that there was a portrait of La Belford in the studio. A nude?"

"Yes," Heimrich said.

"God," Alder said, hopelessly, and went on toward the panel truck. Susan Faye said, "Oh Mr. Alder," and he stopped.

"Could Miss Belford act?" Susan asked.

He looked at her for a moment. Some light from the house was reflected on his face.

"My dear girl," Alder said, "what possible difference could that make?" and went into the truck and drove it off. They watched him go down the drive.

"From another planet," Susan Faye said and Heimrich said, "Yes," and then, "Well—"

"Goodnight, Merton," Susan Faye said.

IV

THE PARKING LOT of the Old Stone Inn was filled. Business normally was good on Saturday nights; this night it seemed excessive. Heimrich found a place for his car and went in through the taproom. Sergeant Forniss loomed in the center of a group of eager men, and one eager woman. He looked at Heimrich over heads and raised his eyebrows and Heimrich nodded. "Here's the captain," Forniss said. The group moved to Heimrich. "M. L.?" the *Times* said. "That right, captain?" That was right. "First name?" the *News* said. "M. L. will do," Heimrich said.

"The sergeant," the *Herald Tribune* said, and spoke accusingly, "the sergeant says it was murder and suicide. You sure about that, captain?"

"That," Heimrich said pleasantly, "is certainly what it looks like. As the sergeant has probably told you."

"The bullets match?" That was the Associated Press.

"One of the bullets was badly damaged," Heimrich said. "They were both from a thirty-eight automatic. There was a thirty-eight on the floor under his hand. Fired twice. But the sergeant's told you that."

"What we want to know," United Press-International said, "are the police sure that it was murder and suicide? Do they write it off?"

"I don't know quite what you mean by write it off," Heimrich said. "Certainly we'll continue the investigation until we're entirely sure. As of now, the facts seem to speak for themselves."

"Hell," the *Mirror* said, expressing a consensus. "A one-day story and—poof. And, it's got everything."

Heimrich smiled slightly. He said he appreciated their feelings.

[50]

"Isn't it possible," the *Times* said, "that further investigation may disclose discrepancies?"

"Anything's possible," Heimrich said.

"Quote you as saying that?"

Heimrich said it seemed to be a harmless enough thing to be quoted as saying. As long as they stopped with that. If there was the implication that the police, officially, were not satisfied—

"Captain," the *News* said, "for my money, you *aren't* satisfied." They all waited.

"I have no reason for thinking Collins didn't shoot Miss Belford and then kill himself," Heimrich said.

"Tried to get her to come back? She wouldn't? He killed her?"

"Now Miss Grady," Heimrich said. "How would I know about that? I wasn't there, naturally."

"The whole movie crowd," the *Mirror* said, "has clammed up on us, captain. Why, if it's the way you say?"

Heimrich didn't know. He assumed they wanted to avoid adverse publicity.

"Or," the *Mirror* said, "know something you're not telling us."

"Gentlemen," Heimrich said. "Miss Grady. If they do know something, I'll try to find out what it is. If it seems to be part of the story, I'll pass it along."

"With deletions," the *Herald Tribune* said, but without animus. Heimrich did not answer that.

"There's a story," the *News* said, "that she was posing in the nude when he shot her."

"She was wearing a swim suit," Heimrich said. "There's nothing to indicate she was posing for him, or had been recently. She was his model years ago, as you probably know. Also his wife."

"She was a lot of guys' wife," the *Mirror* said, sternly. "Frank Dale's, for one. You know that?" The implication was that Heimrich would be unlikely to. Heimrich said he did; said it in his best

[51]

"so what?" tone. "I suppose you know your business," the *Mirror* said, in a voice of doubt.

Heimrich did not answer that either. He said, to the group in general, that that was all he had. Asked, he said they would not, now, be allowed in the house; that after the police were through there, a tour might be arranged. He said that the house had a glass wall and that if any photographers wanted to shoot through the wall he had no objections. He was told that it was dark now, and didn't he know it, and that flashbulbs would reflect in the glass. He said he was sorry.

They began to give him up, then. The *Times*, politely, gave him up first; the others followed. The *Mirror* was last. "In the *Daily Mirror*," the *Mirror* said, "it's going to be mystery shrouds the death of. I can tell you that right now."

"Naturally," Heimrich said, and gestured to Forniss with his head. They went out into the small lobby between taproom and dining room.

"Get anything?" Heimrich said, and they walked to the front of the lobby and stood at a window, from which they could look out into the night; could look under dark trees to Van Brunt Avenue, and the lights of the drugstore across the street, and cars passing between them and the stores.

"Collins picked up the pictures," Forniss said. "Got there about a quarter of four, according to Miss Burns." He considered for a moment. "Miss Myra Burns," he said. "Stayed about half an hour and loaded the pictures in his jeep and drove off. Take him—what? Ten, fifteen minutes to get back to the house. If this Miss Burns is right about times he—"

Probably Myra Burns was right, Heimrich thought. He remembered her. A little bird-like woman who had once been discharged as librarian because the committee—headed by one Orville Phipps, as in those days almost everything in Van Brunt was headed—had objected to her supplying *The Atlantic Monthly* to library patrons, holding *The Atlantic* subversive. Heimrich smiled inwardly, remembering Myra, who hopped so from twig to twig. But probably she was right about times. Anything having to do with the more cultured things of life received Myra Burns's full attention.

"—would have got back around four-thirty," Forniss continued. "So if the doc is right about times, or near right, he had half an hour or so to kill her. Time enough. Only—"

He stopped to let Heimrich finish. Heimrich closed his eyes briefly and nodded his head briefly.

It would have given Collins, certainly, plenty of time to kill before five o'clock, when the examining physician was reasonably sure Peggy Belford had been dead. Heimrich went over it in his mind. Collins had, say, left the house at three-thirty, driven in to pick up his pictures, picked them up, driven back, got home by, say, four-thirty. And killed by five? Time enough, physically; all the time in the world, physically. And conceivably, of course, he could have worked himself up to murder while driving home; brooded himself to violence about whatever made him brood.

"It doesn't give him much time to get worked up to it, does it?" Forniss said, having arrived, apparently, on collision course.

And that, of course, was it. Say, arbitrarily, that Collins had killed his former wife because he had set his hopes high that she was about to return to him and had been told she wasn't. That, perhaps, she had found still another man. Things like that happened. But they did not happen like that—not flatly, logically.

Murder of that sort came as the climax of a great emotional surge; murder like that was the breaking at the crest of a wave of love and hate. This would be particularly true of a man like Brian Collins, if Susan Faye was at all right about the kind of man Collins had been. (If she were really right, of course, no such emotional storm

[53]

would ever have arisen in Collins's self-sufficient mind, however much time was allowed.)

Suppose it had started before he left. That he had brooded over it and made up his mind. Heimrich tried to suppose that—to suppose a man of seething passion turning that passion off arbitrarily, saying, "Excuse me a minute. We'll finish this later. Now I've got to go in and pick up some pictures at the library." And coming back and picking up precisely where, at high pitch, he had left off and— The answer, Heimrich decided, was "Nonsense."

They were left then with a man, who was not the type anyway, coming in at four-thirty, putting his pictures in the studio, working himself up to it—and saying, "Excuse me while I get my gun?"—and killing, all by five? It was not a reasonable place to be left. Of course, the doctor could be wrong. Heimrich doubted it; the doctor had allowed himself leeway. Two hours. Of course, Collins might have killed the girl before he left. The time limits allowed that. And gone in and got his pictures and come back and, belatedly, "worked himself up" to suicide?

"Miss Burns didn't notice anything out of the way about Collins when he came in?" Heimrich asked Forniss. "Like as if he'd just killed somebody."

"No," Forniss said. "He was a little earlier than she had expected was all. He didn't say why. Actually, all he'd said was that he'd be in sometime before six, when the library closes. She kept saying, 'There wasn't any *definite* time.' Also that she couldn't believe it. 'Not in Van *Brunt!*'"

Sergeant Forniss has a heavy voice; he did, nevertheless, manage to suggest Myra Burns, whose conversation was chirped.

"I'm sure she did," Heimrich said. "Charlie, does mystery shroud death of?"

"Nothing proved," Forniss said. "Made up his mind on the way back, could be."

"Nothing proved," Heimrich agreed. "If you had a guest, Charlie. Somebody who'd dropped in during the afternoon for a swim, say. Somebody you had old times to talk over with, perhaps. And, had an errand you had to do. Before six."

Forniss waited; Heimrich spoke slowly.

"Around six," Heimrich said. "Old friends—call it friends—might want to have a drink together. It's the usual time. You might say, 'Look. I've got to drive in to the village and pick up these damn pictures. Can't get out of it. Why don't you have another swim and read a good book or something, and I'll go in and get them and be back by cocktail time and we'll have a drink or two for auld lang syne.'"

"And he finds somebody's shot her while he was away so he kills himself?"

"Now Charlie," Heimrich said. "There's a chance—"

"Captain Heimrich!" The voice was low, almost husky. It was very specially a woman's voice. Heimrich turned.

"You must do something," the girl said. "You can't let this happen. This—*injustice!*"

The voice was too old for her, Heimrich thought, the thought involuntary. She could not be much more than seventeen.

She wore a black dress which hugged a figure worth hugging. She had black hair, loosely curled, hanging almost to her shoulders. She had great dark eyes in an oval face and her skin was unexpectedly white, but with a glow under it. She wore silver earrings and a silver chain around her neck and black shoes with tall heels the diameter of pencils. There was nothing whatever wrong with any part of her, except that she was certainly not over seventeen, and oddly costumed for it, and for a country inn on a summer evening.

Heimrich looked at her and waited. She looked up at him, dark eyes very wide. And, standing so trimly perfect, she turned her right foot so that the toe pointed in. She didn't know that, Heimrich thought. How she would have hated to know that.

"Injustice?" Heimrich said.

"I was in there," she said, in the same husky voice. "Having a drink. Trying not to think. I—heard." On the word "heard" her voice suddenly went up almost an octave. "Heard," she said, darkly, hauling it down again. "They will drag his name into it. Without mercy. Without thought of what it will mean." She paused for a second. "Without *caring*," she said, and there was desolation in the low voice.

There was a great deal of desolation in it. Heimrich felt inadequate to respond appropriately to so much desolation, particularly since he had no idea what she was talking about. Keening about, actually. He thought, further, that they usually wore bobby socks and saddle shoes and sweaters, didn't they? Well, perhaps not sweaters on as warm an evening as this.

"I'm sorry," Heimrich said. "Drag whose name into it, Miss—?"

"Waggoner," she said. "Chris Waggoner. My name means nothing."

Which was, at least for the moment, entirely true.

"Paul Marley's my stepfather," the girl said. "He's the producer of all this."

And this she said crisply, in a matter-of-fact tone, rather as if it were an explanatory footnote.

"I am talking about Francis Dale," she said, in what Heimrich was beginning to recognize as her other voice. "They will crucify him." She paused. "Blazen his name," she said. "Because once, years ago, he had this moment of—weakness."

Heimrich was, for an instant, caught on the thorn of "blazen." He pulled himself loose.

"You must do something," the girl said. "Find some way to stop them."

It seemed improbable that this intensity was concentrated on what he began to suppose it was. But he could think of nothing else.

"You're talking about the reporters?" he said. "The fact that they'll mention that Mr. Dale was at one time Miss Belford's husband?"

"That he was here," she said, intensely. "At the scene of the crime. Don't you *see*? What people will *think*? What it will *do* to him?"

"Scene of the crime?" Heimrich repeated, going to what might be the heart of the matter, if it had a heart. "You mean, the house, Miss Waggoner?"

"Of course not," she said, and said that much in the impatient tone of a girl of seventeen correcting an elder. "Here. In this—whatever it is. Do they call it a town?"

Heimrich decided not to try to explain that. "I can't," he said, "control the newspapers. But I doubt that they'll insinuate anything about Mr. Dale. Just what is it you're afraid of?"

"An artist," she said, and now was again the—Heimrich sought a term. Actress, certainly. In tragic role, beyond a doubt. "A great artist. Sensitive. He must be protected."

Assuming she was still talking about Francis Dale, Heimrich considered briefly. A good actor and a veteran at it, beyond a doubt. A man of quivering sensibility, who would be "crucified" because his name was mentioned in accounts of his former wife's murder? Heimrich doubted it. He had seen Dale several times since the company had been on location in Van Brunt. Dale had not looked like a man who quivered readily.

"Among other things," Heimrich said to the girl in black, who waited actively—who was all a tragic, waiting girl, "among other things, they won't insinuate anything that might give anyone grounds for suit. As a practical matter, Miss Waggoner. Aside from the fact that they aren't particularly malicious people. The reporters, I mean."

She sighed, deeply. Her sigh was recognition of the hopelessly obtuse. She turned away, shaking her head so that the dark hair swayed around it.

"Unless," Heimrich said, "there is more than I know about at the moment. Something that would involve Mr. Dale."

That brought her back.

"What could there be?" she demanded. "Years ago he was sorry for Peggy. She took him in—all right, she took him in. Not the first one or the last. But he never loved her. He couldn't have. So why would he—" She caught herself. "Do anything?" she said.

"I don't know," Heimrich said. "Why are you afraid he did?"

"I'm not," she said. "I'm *not*." And she was a girl of seventeen, who might have been wearing bobby socks and saddle shoes, or whatever they were wearing this year, when they were seventeen. "Why do you say that?"

"Now Miss Waggoner," Heimrich said. "Everything indicates that this is a simple case. That Mr. Collins killed Miss Belford and shot himself. That nobody else was involved. So—why do you feel that Mr. Dale needs—" He hesitated. "Protection?" he said.

"That's ridiculous," the girl said, resuming the superiority of youth. "He is strong. Sensitive, but strong. And gentle and kind and—" She stopped abruptly. "I suppose," she said, "you think I've got a crush on him."

He smiled down at her, the smile answering.

"And," she said, "that I was jealous of that Peggy Belford."

He continued to look at her, smiling down at her, and saw the flicker in her eyes—the flicker which, he supposed, indicated a sudden realization that she had given herself away.

"She was throwing herself at him," the girl said. "Getting her claws in. Just for the fun of it."

"And he?"

"He's older," she said. "He must be—" She paused. "About your age," she said. Heimrich mentally blinked at that, and was somewhat taken aback. Dale was, he was pretty certain, fifteen years older. Fifteen anyway. "At that age," Miss Chris Waggoner said, "men become susceptible. To scheming little—" She stopped with that. She did not, Heimrich supposed, wish to offend his aged ears. He wondered where she had read about the susceptibility of middle-aged men to scheming little—schemers.

"There wasn't anything really,", she said. "He just isn't the sort of man who would—who wouldn't be unkind. Even to somebody like Peggy."

Who wouldn't, Heimrich supposed, tell a scheming little schemer to go peddle her papers; wouldn't brush such a one off. Heimrich considered the girl he had seen lying dead; seen pictured. Not a girl any man, middle-aged or otherwise, would casually brush off, if offered.

"I shouldn't have done this at all," Chris Waggoner said. "I've just—given you ideas. All the wrong ideas."

Which was, at least partly, true. The ideas need not, of course, be wrong.

"Anyway," Chris said, with resolution—and with the hoarse throb back in her young voice. "Anyway, I know where he was all yesterday afternoon. He was with me. We were—" She hesitated. Fatally. "Out in his car," she said, with even greater resolution.

"All right," Heimrich said. "Then there's nothing to worry about, is there?"

Her eyes flickered again. But she did not return to that, at least not directly.

"Captain Heimrich," she said, "Brian Collins wasn't up there. At his house. At least, part of the time he wasn't. Did you know that?"

Heimrich nodded his head and she said, "Oh," and was a little deflated. "How did you know?" Heimrich said.

She had gone to the library to look at the pictures. "There's nothing to *do* here," she said, defensively. "Not that I'm not interested in art," she said, defending the other side of the net. She had been there when Brian Collins had come in to get his paintings.

She had known him, apparently?

Two or three days before, he had had several of them up for—well, call it a swimming party. "Nobody else around here seems to have a pool," she said, in wonderment at quaint native customs. Apparently he had told his former wife—she supposed he and "that Peggy" must have "got together" earlier; "that Peggy" wasn't one to let any presentable man lie around unused—to come up any time and bring any friends she wanted to. She had met Brian Collins then, which was all there was to her knowing him. It was enough to enable her to recognize him at the library, of course.

When had he been there? Her times accorded well enough with those given by Myra Burns. "It was earlier Francis and I were out in his car," she said, quickly, not so much covering that as drawing a slight veil across it. So, Brian Collins was away from the house for some time anyway and— She stopped.

"And I wanted to *help* Francis," she said, with a slight wail in her voice. "Not that there's any need but—"

"Now Miss Waggoner," Heimrich said. "I knew Collins was away from the house for an hour or so. And that Miss Belford may have, for that period, been there alone. So you haven't done Mr. Dale any harm. Or, anyone else. Speaking of that, do you know whether anyone else knew Mr. Collins was in town this afternoon?"

"Anybody might have seen him," she said. "I don't know. We'd all come back from that barn up the river. Paul knocked it off for the afternoon. There are only a couple more scenes anyway and he wanted to shoot them in the morning. Because of the shadows."

"Miss Waggoner," Heimrich said, "are you in this picture?"

"You think he'd let me do anything with her around?" the girl said, bitterly, if unclearly. Heimrich momentarily closed his eyes.

"Paul," she said. "That stepfather of mine. He had it as bad as anybody. Peggyitis. You think she'd get anything but a walk-on if it weren't for that?" Heimrich opened his eyes. "Didn't you ever see her notices?" Chris demanded. "Not that the critics know anything and most of them hate movies anyway. You can tell that by—"

Heimrich had, once or twice before, heard actors on the subject of critics. They can go on a long time, if left to it.

"She got bad notices?" he said.

"Oh," Chris said, "they all said she was beautiful. All right, I guess she was. If you like them that way, and men seem to. Even a boy like George. But act? Figure and face of a statue by Pheidias, one of them said, and about the same mobility. And somebody else said she had two facial expressions—pout and not-pout."

"I take it," Heimrich said, "that Mr. Marley—your stepfather— didn't agree with that estimate?"

"Captain," Chris said, "I don't say he's not a good producer. Doesn't know his job. A heel but—" She stopped. "I suppose," she said, "you think I oughtn't to say that? Ought to show what-you-may- call-it? Filial respect?" Her tone made the expression ridiculous. "It was my mother married him," she said, and spoke with sudden bitterness. "Not me."

Heimrich waited.

"As for Paul thinking she could act," Chris said. She was her age, now, even if not dressed for it. "Nobody thought that."

"Then?"

"What I said. Peggyitis. Everybody had to carry her. Even Georgie-Porgie." Heimrich looked blank. "George Latham," she said. "In the picture he's Francis's son and they're both in love with Peggy the innocent milkmaid. It's a real corny script. Either Peggyitis or she knows where somebody buried the body. Or—something."

A jealous child, presumably; a child unwilling to wait for growth —an impatient child. Which accounted for the dress; the too-heavy earrings. Why, Heimrich wondered, did he then feel a kind of amused tenderness toward her, a friendly sympathy? Not only because, even now, she was nearly beautiful, and might—would almost certainly—come closer. The kid was intelligent; only the intelligent are likely, when very young, to make themselves appear so foolish.

"Your mother's dead?" Heimrich asked, not knowing precisely why he wondered. She had said nothing about that.

"She's dead," Chris said. "Why did you ask that?" She looked up at him and for the first time there was a smile on her soft lips. "Because you think I need a mother's guidance?"

"Now Miss Waggoner."

"Maybe I do," she said. "I come rushing at you. All protective and—anyway, all protective. And what comes of it? You pump me dry, don't you?"

"Have I?"

He smiled at her.

"As dry," she said. "All the same, it isn't fair for Francis to—to be hurt. She wasn't worth it." He looked down at her. "Oh," she said, "I know she's dead and—" She stopped. She said, "Well," and turned and started toward the taproom.

"Miss Waggoner," Heimrich said and she stopped. "You said you were having a drink," he said. "Of what?"

For a moment she was, again, a woman of the world, in black dress, haughty in the face of impertinence. And then, with nothing intermediate, she grinned at him, grinned like an imp, not caring how she looked.

"I don't like you," she said, with a kind of pleased delight in her voice. "Not at all. Coke. Coke. *Daddy.*"

And went.

"I don't," Sergeant Forniss remarked, "get them. Was she up to something?"

"Several things, possibly," Heimrich said. "Including the things she said she was up to. About Dale. We'll have to talk to Dale, of course."

"To everybody," Forniss agreed. "Only—where is it going to get us? Because if we can't find something the matter with the way it looks, with the physical setup, where are we? Because no D.A.'s going to buck the obvious."

"I know," Heimrich said.

"Anybody else," Forniss said. "Saying there is anybody, would have to come and dangle his paws and say, 'Please, I did it.'"

"I know, Charlie," Heimrich said. "It's all very difficult."

V

FRANCIS DALE TOOK it that the police were not entirely satisfied. Francis Dale was a tall lean man, with a compact brown face and crinkles at the corners of his eyes. His eyes were blue. There was gray becomingly at his temples. He wore a brown goatee. He sat, in polo shirt and walking shorts, on a sofa in The Suite, the capital letters being applied, when it was mentioned, by the Old Stone Inn. He looked at Heimrich speculatively and pulled at the beard. "Damn thing itches," he said. "Why aren't you satisfied, captain?"

Francis Dale had a deep voice, and used it with care. He had strong brown hands and, beard pulled sufficiently, used one of them to lift a long glass. He said, "Won't change your mind?" and smiled pleasantly. He was, Heimrich knew—everybody knew—in his middle fifties; he looked it and didn't look it.

He wouldn't, Heimrich said, want to put it quite so definitely. There was routine to be gone through. "Just a few routine questions, m'lady," Dale said, in a voice suddenly very British. "I played that role once, a long time ago. At the Empire. Beautiful house, the Empire. M'lady turned out to be guilty as hell, as I recall it."

He was relaxed, sipped at his drink.

"I suppose," he said, "you've got reporters in your hair?"

"Naturally," Heimrich said. "Considering."

Dale nodded. He said, "It's a sad thing, captain. She was such a very pretty child. Was living with such—enthusiasm. A bit too much, perhaps. At least it—" He paused and sipped and appeared to reflect. "I found it so," he said. "During our brief association. During the time I was playing the rather inert role of steppingstone. I assume that's what you're interested in, captain? If you think Collins didn't

[64]

kill her? Did I? Overcome by—by youthful passion?" He smiled, pleasantly. He shook his handsome head. He said, "No, captain."

"Did you see Mr. Collins in the village this afternoon?" Heimrich asked him. "That's the sort of routine I'm interested in at the moment."

"No," Dale said. "If that's what you really want to know. If you want to know where I was most of the afternoon, which I imagine is the point, I was here. From about three until around six. Sleeping, most of the time. Zersk is a great man for dawn shots. With people in them, unfortunately. Got back here around one. Had a couple of drinks and lunch with Paul—Paul Marley, that is—and young George. Talked about tomorrow's schedule, after which, thank God, I can shave."

"Not," Heimrich said, "out driving with Miss Waggoner?"

Dale put his drink down on the cocktail table.

"Now what," he said, "ever put that in—" And stopped. "Oh my God," he said. "Chris, again. From babies with—" Again he stopped.

"Crushes?" Heimrich said, when Dale did not go on. And Dale nodded, slowly.

"She is," Dale said, "a very sweet child. Very sweet and very young and very foolish. I could be her father, captain. If I had been sufficiently precocious, her grandfather. Assuming an offspring equally impetuous. Cradles are safe from me, captain." He looked at Heimrich and narrowed his eyes slightly and then, suddenly, smiled. "And don't," he said, "cite Peggy Belford. I doubt if our Peggy ever had a cradle." He sobered; his face changed, became another face. "The poor kid," he said. "I keep forgetting, somehow. Chris was—what? Protecting me from your evil suspicions?"

"Partly," Heimrich said. "Partly, she wanted me to gag the press. She seems to think that's possible. So that your name would not be —the word she used was 'blazened.'"

"She had on that black dress?" Dale said. "And the deep dark voice?"

Heimrich nodded his head.

"The baby," Dale said. "Of course, she'll get over it. They all do." He smiled then, and seemed to smile at himself. "More's the pity," he added, as if to himself. "An occupational hazard, captain. And, at the same time, part of the—well, of the operation. The company's. But, mine too. I don't deny that. Box office is as the female does. Or, dreams. And probably you think I'm quite—insufferable. An old goat. At the moment, with beard to match."

He had not been looking at Heimrich as he spoke. Now, abruptly, he did.

"Now Mr. Dale," Heimrich said. "Why should I?"

"The word's been used," Dale said, and now he grinned at Heimrich. "By husbands, from time to time. Husbands of women I'd never met. What's come over them, do you suppose? Why don't they pick on somebody their age? They used to. But, I can't complain. Several of my contemporaries can't complain, either." He drank again. "In this case," he said, "the case of our little Chris, I've been doing what I could. Because of one thing and another. Gertrude's death, for one thing. And—Chris is real. A real girl, here and now. Not somebody who says, 'I'll treasure it forever, Mr. Dale,' and shoves an autograph book."

When he quoted "somebody" he was, for that instant, in voice, almost in appearance (which was absurd) a teen-age girl with book and pencil.

It could not, Heimrich thought, be contended that Francis Dale was not, among other things, an actor. Tall and lean and handsome, and an actor too. So—

"What have you been doing, Mr. Dale?" Heimrich asked and, on being looked at blankly, added, "To discourage Miss Waggoner. If that was what you meant."

"Oh," Dale said. "Paying attention to Peggy. Letting Chris see that I thought she was a child and—" And he stopped. He said, "My God!"

"Making her jealous," Heimrich said. "She is, Mr. Dale. Or—was."

"Captain," Dale said. "This man Collins shot Peggy. And killed himself. That's—all over the place. Why aren't you people satisfied with that?"

He had come full circle. But, where he had seemed only a little amused before, even when he proposed himself as a suspect, he was not at all amused now. "She's a child," Dale said, angrily. "Got childish notions, dramatizes things. But—a child. A sweet child."

"Now Mr. Dale," Heimrich said. "You're jumping at things. Who was the Gertrude you mentioned? Chris's mother?"

"I don't see—" Dale said and shrugged and said, "All right. Maybe you know what you're after. Chris's mother. A damn good actress in her day, which wasn't far from mine. A damned nice person. I'll never know why she did it."

"Did what?"

"Took an overdose about eighteen months ago," Dale said. "There was enough about it in the papers." He considered. "In the Los Angeles papers, anyway," he said. "Gertrude Fletcher?"

Heimrich shook his head.

"Her real name," Dale said. "Gives you an idea how good she was to get where she did with a name like that. Then she married Waggoner and retired and had Chris and Waggoner died. And then, seven-eight years ago, she married Paul. And did a comeback for one picture and got nice notices—nice enough—and then a year and a half ago—" He shrugged. "It was a damn bad thing for Chris," he said. "Her mother meant a lot to her. And she doesn't—" He stopped. He said this was beside the point.

"Like her stepfather," Heimrich said. "She told me. He's a good deal younger than Chris's mother was, I'd imagine."

"Fifteen years or thereabouts," Dale said. "One of our boy wonders."

"Is he?"

"Good at his job? Very."

"Mr. Dale," Heimrich said, "was Miss Belford a good actress?"

He was told he asked the damnedest unrelated things. He was asked whether that was a question Chris had raised.

"Yes," Heimrich said, and waited.

"What difference does it make now?"

"Now Mr. Dale," Heimrich said. "I haven't any idea, really. Was she?"

"They paid to see her," Dale said. "She was worth seeing, you know. She could wear clothes, and give the impression she wasn't wearing them, if you know what I mean. She had a hell of a lot of vitality, and it showed on the screen."

"Could she act?"

"All right," Dale said, "if it matters a damn—not for peanuts. She drove Tony Zersk crazy. She drove a lot of directors crazy. Now and then she drove me crazy, if you want to know. And—what's the idea? Somebody kill her because she wasn't much of an actress and drove directors and actors crazy? If that sort of thing went on, half the babes in Hollywood would be as full of holes as sieves. More than half."

"But," Heimrich said, "Mr. Marley, and other producers apparently, gave her parts."

"Sure. I told you why. But, you saw her, man."

"Not alive," Heimrich said. "However—"

"Take my word for it," Dale said. "Sure, I was a steppingstone. And, believe it or not, knew it at the time. And—didn't give a damn." He considered. "For a few months, anyway," he said.

What precisely, Heimrich wanted to know, did Dale mean by "steppingstone?" Dale would have thought that obvious. Also, and again, what was all this about? He looked at Heimrich, his eyes narrowed.

"Listen," he said, "you're not playing along with the newspapers on this, are you? I mean—I've heard of policemen who don't mind publicity. And aren't above making mysteries because mysteries make better newspaper stories and—" He paused. Heimrich had closed his eyes. "Skip it," Dale said.

Heimrich opened his eyes.

"Where there aren't any mysteries," Heimrich said. "Mr. Dale, we have trouble enough with things as they are. As for what it's all about—it helps to know as much as we can find out about people involved. Particularly about people who get killed. I take it you meant Miss Belford felt there would be certain advantages to being your wife?"

"Of course," Dale said. "It sticks out—stuck out then. Like it or not, I'm a star. Box office. Which gives me a certain amount of influence. Peggy—felt she could use influence. So—"

"A trade," Heimrich said.

Dale fingered his itchy beard. He said, a little wearily, that Heimrich could call it that, if he wanted to call it that. If he found it simpler to call it that.

"Now Mr. Dale," Heimrich said. "I don't imply—"

Dale waved a hand. He said, again, "Skip it, captain. You don't have to approve."

"That," Heimrich said, "doesn't come into it. You helped her along?"

"To a degree. Suggested her name here and there, for parts she could handle. And she did well enough, for a girl who couldn't act. And, come to that, knew it. She's—she was bright enough, in her way. Didn't think she was going to be another Lynn or Helen. Far's I know, didn't particularly want to be. More the diamonds-are-

[69]

a-girl's-best-friend type." He looked at Heimrich and smiled faintly. "I suppose you think we're an odd menagerie," he said.

"I gather," Heimrich said, "that Mr.—" He paused, remembering. "The automobile dealer," he said, and remembered. "Mr. Fielding. That he was the diamond type?"

"Fielding," Dale said, "was more the alimony type, as it turned out. I imagine it ran to diamonds." He leaned forward suddenly. "You don't have to pay alimony when they're dead," he said. The idea, evidently, pleased him. "If you decide not to settle for Collins."

"Thanks," Heimrich said. "That's very—"

The door of The Suite's living room opened with a slight explosion.

"M. G.'s fit to be—" a man said, his voice also explosive, and stopped with that and added, "Oh!"

"Captain Heimrich, Paul," Francis Dale said. "The local police. Seems he doesn't altogether buy our friend Collins. And is—shopping. This is Paul Marley, captain. The producer of *The Last Patroon*. By the way, do you like the title, captain?"

"I think," Heimrich said gravely, "that it lacks something. Fit to be what, Mr. Marley? Tied, I suppose?"

Marley was a big man with a big head and he had a deep voice. By the time he was fifty, Heimrich thought—and that he was some ten years from that—he might well be a big fat man. He had wavy blond hair. (When Marley had been thirty, Heimrich thought, he must have looked like an unmarred heavyweight. Or football player.)

"Tied," Marley agreed, deeply. "What does he mean you're not satisfied with Collins?"

Heimrich said that went too far. He again went through the routine about routine. Dale lifted the bottle from the cocktail table and Marley said, "God yes," and went to it and poured from it. "Still sitting out?" Dale said, politely, and Heimrich nodded.

"Did you," Dale said, "tell M. G. that you were through with her? Except for a couple of long shots you can fake?"

"Obviously," Marley said. "Kept on yelling at me. You know how he is about dead ones."

"I know," Dale said, and turned to Heimrich. "M. G. Drisken," he said, "has a fetish about actors being dead when their films are released. Thinks audiences tend to puddle up seeing dead people so alive on the screen. And he's got a couple of Peggy's in cans. In addition to the one we're finishing now."

"You mean," Heimrich said, "that he won't release the pictures? Because Miss Belford's dead?"

Both men looked at him in astonishment. They looked at each other.

"I said," Dale said, "that he had a fetish. I didn't say he was a lunatic." He turned to Paul Marley. "I suppose," he said, "he blames you?"

"Who else?" Marley said, in his very deep voice, and sighed deeply. "If I can't keep my actors alive, he'll have to look around for somebody who can. Also, who the hell is this guy Collins, and what does he think he is? And that I was the one who insisted on having Peggy in it, although he'd told me a hundred times she was more trouble than she was worth."

"Were you?" Heimrich asked. "Had he?"

The two men looked at each other again. Dale shrugged.

"M. G.," Dale said, "is a brilliant man in the industry. He is given to getting excited. He didn't particularly object to Peggy in the part. Both Paul and I thought she would be quite satisfactory in it." He smiled faintly. "It was not," he said, "what they call a demanding part. She looked pretty. She was a milkmaid. Early on I, the last patroon, come on her bathing in what I suppose is a mill-pond. Very pretty indeed. I can see her, I might add, much more clearly than

[71]

the audience can. In view of the Code. Her big scene is when she chooses George instead of me. Nothing beyond her powers."

"George Latham," Marley said. "Juvenile lead. Which reminds me. You the policeman my stepdaughter was talking to?"

"Yes," Heimrich said.

"That kid," Marley said. "About what a bitch Peggy was, I suppose?"

"She didn't tell you?"

Marley looked astonished.

"Tell me?" he said. "She wouldn't, as they say, give me the time of day. She glided out of the bar, leaving George flat, and after a while glided back in and said, in that voice of hers, 'The police have been questioning me.' I was a couple of tables away with Tony Zersk. Her voice carries. That tragic queen voice."

Marley, when he quoted his stepdaughter, himself used a very special voice—a voice with Chris's own throb in it. Another actor, obviously.

"She hoped," Heimrich said, "that I could do something to lessen the publicity."

"By God," Marley said, "she had something there. For once." He looked at Heimrich intently, measuringly. "M. G. would be pleased," he said. "Very pleased."

"I told her, of course," Heimrich said, "that that was quite impossible."

"But damn it," Marley said. "It's open and shut. Everybody says that. You've got some reason for saying it isn't? Something wrong with the way it looks?"

Heimrich went, once more, through the routine about routine. It didn't sound too convincing to his own ears. He, however, asked questions to prove it.

Had Marley known that Brian Collins was in the village, and hence away from the house he died in, for some time that afternoon?

Marley had not. Had he known that Miss Belford was going to Collins's house to swim in his pool?

"Sure," Marley said, and looked at Francis Dale and said, "You heard her too, Frank. And Tony did and probably Georgie-Porgie." (Heimrich felt sympathy for George Latham, whom he had not yet met.)

Dale nodded his becomingly silvered head. He moved it slowly, with control.

"When we finished," Marley said. "It was a little after noon— when we finished she said that she was going over and use Brian's pool and that if anybody else wanted to come along she was sure Brian wouldn't mind. Nobody did."

"Because the rest of you thought Collins might mind?"

Heimrich was looked at in surprise by both tall men.

"Why would he?" Marley asked. "Anyway, he'd more or less given us carte blanche."

And Francis Dale smiled, then let the smile expand to a chuckle.

"What Paul really means," he said, "is 'What pool wouldn't we honor?' We get that way, captain."

And, saying that, Dale convinced Heimrich that he, for one, hadn't got that way at all. Unless— It didn't matter.

"A little after noon," Heimrich said. "She'd have to come back— she was staying here at the Inn?"

She had been.

"And changed, and driven over to the Collins place. By the way, in a Buick wagon?"

"Mine," Marley said. "Damn it all, I'd forgotten about it. Is it still up at the Collins place?"

It was. Would it be all right for one of them to go up and get it? It would, whenever they liked. Miss Belford had borrowed the car? She had. That is— Marley looked at Dale and shrugged.

"What it comes to," Dale said, "is that we more or less use any car

[73]

handy. The station wagon. The panel truck. A—an aborted sense of mine and thine, captain. What Peggy actually said, as I recall it, was, 'I'll take the wagon if nobody else wants it.' And did."

Heimrich nodded his head. He closed his eyes momentarily. "A little after noon" might, he supposed, mean anything. He asked. It seemed to mean about twelve-twenty to Dale; twelve forty-five was more like it to Marley. Twenty minutes to drive to the Inn. How long to change? He could only guess. Lunch? He asked. Neither man knew. They had not seen her lunching at the Inn, but they had been in the taproom. She might have been in the main dining room. Equally, she might have got a sandwich somewhere else—on the road down from location.

There was no way to pin it down.

"I don't," Marley said, "see what the hell difference it makes."

"I don't know that it makes—" Heimrich said, and somebody knocked at the door and Dale said, "Come in." Sergeant Forniss came in. He said, "Got a minute, captain?"

Which meant, of course, that Forniss had come up with something.

VI

WHILE HE HAD been there, it had been possible, with some effort, to keep it pushed to the back of the mind; to wall it off there; to, in a fashion, draw a screen over the picture. It had been possible, to some degree, to think of murder in the abstract, as a problem to be solved. (Assuming always that there was a problem.) After he drove off, that had no longer been possible.

Then the picture came back—the ugly picture of violent death. One read of such things and, inevitably, imagined the way they had looked. But this was as one imagined, with horror in the mind rather than in the senses, the deaths far away, of famine, of thousands unknown, to a degree unreal. Even photographs were not the same —photographs of emaciated faces and bloated bodies if death came from famine; of the torn victims of accidental death or of death by murder. For one thing, such pictures are edited for flinching minds. "The body of one of the victims may be seen in the left foreground," but what is seen is a sheet over something—the shape of something. Which, Susan Faye thought, is the way it should always be, and blood should be only a word. Not something seeped deeply into a chair. A "head wound" should be a term of description, not—not the hideous thing it is.

With him there, she had been able—almost able—to think of the violent deaths of Peggy Belford and Brian Collins as death in the abstract; as if, she thought, they had bled sawdust. (It was odd that the girl had bled so little. Or wasn't it odd? She didn't know.) She supposed this was because, with him there, she could to some degree share the attitude which it was essential he adopt. Bodies have been

[75]

broken. Hence, the law has been broken. One finds out how, by whom.

She knew him too well to think that detachment went deep in Merton Heimrich. Once or twice, when he had talked about cases he was working on—cases of which she knew no more than he told her—she had realized, and each time with momentary surprise, how deeply he felt about them. Possibly, she thought—had thought those times and thought again now—it was because of a fundamental rejection of violence, almost a loathing of it, that he had decided to follow the trade he followed. She would ask him sometime.

With the trade, certainly, had come an ability to insulate himself —to pretend, on the surface of the mind, that bodies bleed sawdust; that murder is not a hideous picture which can fill the mind, but a puzzle to be solved. And, when he was with her, she could somehow share that insulation, try with him to work out the problem.

And now he had gone and left her with the picture in her mind. She could look at anything—look at the frypan to be scraped, put to soak—and see a slender girl in a bathing suit, one knee gracefully lifted, dead eyes staring at a ceiling; see a man she had talked to only hours before slumped with a great black hole in his head and blood all around him. She scraped blood from the frypan, not what remained of lamb curry. She—

Damn the man, Susan Faye thought, quite irrationally. (Because I was the one who led us to it, not he.) To go off to see people, talk to people, work on his puzzle, and leave me here to remember—to vividly remember blood. To feel the beginning of nausea because wherever I look—

The thing was, of course, to put it out of her mind. People were always saying that—"Just put it out of your mind. Don't let yourself think about it." So—think about what, then? About a large doleful dog who had followed her into the kitchen and watched, hopelessly, while she threw food away? "You know you won't eat anything with curry in it," Susan Faye told Colonel. "Why do you pretend?"

Colonel sighed. There was little about Colonel, at best, to uplift the spirits. When he saw food disappear anywhere except into dog, Colonel was not at his best.

Very well, if it could not be put out of the mind, think of it as a puzzle. That was, certainly, the only sensible thing to do. The other was—indulging the emotions. Chilling one's own blood, which did no good to anyone. Think of it as a puzzle. If it was a puzzle. Decide, clearly, why—unclearly—her mind had rejected what was obviously true: that Brian Collins, in what must have been a moment of uncontrollable desperation, had killed a girl he must have loved enough to hate. Why had she rejected what was obvious?

She had told him—the great oaf, the dear slow oaf, the bump on a log—that it was because what Collins seemed to have done did not jibe with what she knew about Brian Collins, with the kind of man she was sure he was. And the great oaf had listened, been kind enough, gentle enough, to pretend for them both that what she said made sense. (I do wish, Susan thought, in parenthesis, that he wouldn't be quite so *damn* gentle.) He had even pretended to believe, for both of them, that what he called the "outline" of a person, detected quickly, had some validity.

I know better, Susan said, wandering out onto the terrace—followed gloomily by Colonel—and of course he knows better. Collins was a man; he was even, probably, sometimes a violent man. Abrupt —she herself had said that about him, before any of this had happened. And certainly one cannot tell from a few meetings, from a few words of no consequence. One's own experience should tell one that. People, even people one had known well for years, sometimes did the most unlikely, the most inexplicable, things. She knew that as well as anybody. Honor students at high school, highly regarded by one and all, now and then killed their parents, in fits of exasperation. And mousy little doctors killed their wives and buried them deep, and the neighbors assured one another that they just couldn't believe it.

So—there was nothing to the contention that Brian Collins simply had not been the type. Erase that, rub it from the mind. And—what was left?

Susan lighted a cigarette and looked up at the sky—it was beginning to haze over—and waited to see what was left.

What was left was, quite simply, the abiding conviction that what appeared to have happened at Brian Collins's house was not what had actually happened. Aside, obviously, from the fact that two people had been shot to death.

You, Susan Faye said to Susan Faye, are a silly female, a ridiculous female. Which is an insult to your intelligence. You, Susan Faye told herself sternly, are having intuition. It doesn't become you.

Thus admonished, she gave her mind a moment finally to erase this ridiculous conviction. And, resolutely, her mind declined the opportunity. Also, her mind said, a little smugly, It isn't an intuition. So, face it, Susan Faye.

If not an intuition, then something was wrong with the picture. (Not the "picture"; don't open the mind to a picture. Not again.) With, then, the setup. Consider the setup, if you're so sure something is wrong with it. Consider it objectively. Get yourself a drink and sit here calmly and consider objectively. She went into the house—doing something with the body, and especially with the hands, is always a good idea—and mixed herself a very mild gin-and-tonic and brought it back out to the chaise built for two. Now—

Brian Collins was a man of violent emotions, violent jealousy. Assume that, since you do not know he wasn't. He wanted a very pretty young woman, most enticingly under-clothed—and hadn't she known it, the little vixen—to return to him and she had—what? Laughed? That might easily have done it. So he shot her. And—she sprawled. Most hideously. (And don't make a picture of it, for the love of God!)

And—it had been easier to kill than to see the hideous results of killing, to see beauty made grotesque. The one might be thought of as punishment, the other was—sacrilege, an offense against the idea of beauty, the conception of beauty.

So—go first and put the portrait on an easel, restore, in semblance, beauty destroyed. Look long at it, try to remember it; replace with it what sprawled on a tile floor; fill the mind with it. (A mind, of course, no longer rational, no longer sane.) Go back, then, and try— the mind surging, not longer really a mind—to repair, to make amends. Move the slender, unresponsive body. (And remember in what manner, once, it had responded? Susan shivered, drank from her glass.) Give it the decency of comeliness; administer the last rites to beauty.

Was it all too—fantastic? Too macabre, too Gothic? Was that what was wrong with it?

She considered, lying back, looking up at the slowly hazing sky. (Tomorrow probably would be muggy; an enervating day.) Collins had been a painter; a man who sought to create beauty. A man, who, more intensely than most, saw beauty and, conversely, ugliness; more intensely than most, responded to both. Colors were clearer to him than to most. (As, Susan thought, they are to me; it is neither virtue nor fault, but a way of being.) Colors and forms in —in everything. It was conceivable that, in such a man, the knowledge that he had destroyed beauty might override almost anything else. Might, indeed, become, in a reeling mind, a shield against the less bearable knowledge that he had destroyed life. Repair the one; absolve one's self from the other. Perhaps.

Not, then, that the conception was too fantastic. Assume that— assume that it was not the fantasy which snagged the mind. Then, something in the physical aspect, something quite matter of fact?

The weapon in the wrong place? Some mechanical impossibility? No, Susan thought. Merton—how could I ever have thought of calling him Ricky? Like a band leader?—would have seen anything like that. I am no match for him in things like that. So?

So, you're not up to it, Susan Faye. Face it, you've gone intuitional. Probably it is even simpler—probably, because Brian Collins was a painter and a pretty good one and you have a thing about painting, you don't want it to be the way it looks. Probably it is as simple, and as silly, as that.

On the terrace beside her Colonel made a sad dog sound.

"All right," Susan said to the great dog. "You want me to settle down, so you can settle down. Come on, then."

She got up quickly. Colonel groaned and ambled to his feet. They went into the house. Colonel went to the room in which the small god should be, sniffed, faced Susan and wept.

"A goof of a dog," Susan said. "Come on, then."

He followed her into her bedroom. He watched her undress. When she was stretched on the bed he sighed deeply and thudded to the floor beside the bed. Almost at once he began to snore.

Susan slept fitfully and dreamed much. She dreamed in color, which was not unusual for her, since to a considerable degree she lived in color. Most of her dreams were red. Once she wakened herself by speaking and, which is uncommon, heard her own words. She had said, quite distinctly, "Bad color."

Colonel snorted.

"Go to sleep," Susan Faye said, and had another try at it herself. And now, for some reason, she slept more deeply and dreams did not waken her. It was as if she had taken a sedative which had quietened her mind.

***

Sergeant Forniss was already at breakfast when Heimrich got

down to the Inn's dining room at a little after eight. He was alone in the big room; eight o'clock Sunday morning is not a favorite time for breakfast. Forniss was eating bacon and scrambled eggs. Heimrich pulled out a chair and sat down opposite him.

"Dermal nitrate's positive," Forniss said, in a tone he might have used to report that his eggs were overcooked. Heimrich said, "Oh," and spread a napkin. "On both hands," Forniss said, and Heimrich said, "Oh" on a different note. He added that that was one of the things the matter with the damn thing.

The dermal nitrate test, the coating of hands, with paraffin, the application to the hardened paraffin of Lunge's reagent, should have told them whether Brian Collins had in fact fired the pistol which had killed two people. That was what it was for; that was why it was part of the routine. Nitrate particles from powder explosion show up blue when brought into contact with Lunge's reagent. So, unfortunately, do nitrate particles from other sources.

"Had a garden, I suppose," Heimrich said and to the waitress, "Orange juice and soft-boiled eggs please, Gretchen."

Forniss said, "Yep." He said that it was a vegetable garden and that Collins had apparently been cultivating it the morning before and, from the looks, hoeing in fertilizer. Which contains nitrates; which grinds into hands. The dermal nitrate test does not discriminate among nitrates.

"Too bad," Heimrich said, and "Thank you," to Gretchen for orange juice and coffee.

"Juries like nitrate tests," Forniss said, somewhat gloomily. "Science. Nothing like science. However much the D.A. was to talk about fertilizer."

"I know," Heimrich said. "Odd she was so business-like, isn't it?"

It was not precisely a change of subject; it was a variant on the only subject in either mind.

And it was odd; it was that oddity which Forniss had, the night

[81]

before, come to mention. It was that oddity which had led them to say goodnight to a handsome actor and a large producer with a voice of almost unexampled depth and heavy power, and to postpone the questioning of a young actor unfortunately called "Georgie-Porgie" by those who knew him well, and a director known as Tony Zersk—and, it was to be presumed, others. First things first. Clear things up, if you can, as they arise. Clear up a man named Roland Fielding.

"Take it one way," Forniss said, "she was a business woman."

"I hope they're right," Gretchen said, of eggs. Heimrich cracked an egg into its cup. "Exactly," he said and Gretchen departed, pleased. A man about his boiled eggs, the captain was.

"A diamonds-are-a-girl's-best-friend girl," Heimrich said. "What Dale called her. All the same—carbons. Not that it wasn't sensible of her."

"Helpful, too," Forniss said. "Maybe."

Peggy Belford had had a large room at the Old Stone Inn, a room befitting a featured player, and also a girl with a wardrobe. "You'd think," a trooper told Forniss, when he made his find and reported, "she was going on a trip around the world or something." The wardrobe was not, however, the subject of the report; it was merely a minor reason for astonishment.

The subject of the report was a portable typewriter, prettily pink. The subject of the report was a cardboard filing case, containing—among other things still being checked on—carbon copies of a number of letters written on the pretty pink typewriter. Finally, the subject of the report was one of the letter copies. Forniss had read it and had said, mildly, "Well, well," and gone to tell Heimrich.

Now Heimrich said, "Let's see it again, Charlie," and Charlie passed it across the table. "Fingerprinted," he said. "Hers." Heimrich read it. It was nicely typed, nicely spaced, very business-like. It was dated a week earlier. It read:

"Dear Rollie: I'm too, too sorry to hear about these financial reverses of yours and how difficult it's become to keep up the payments. And, Rollie dear, I couldn't care less. Really I couldn't.

"Because, Rollie dear, two thousand dollars a month is what it says and my copy of the court order is all locked away in a little safe deposit box, and I haven't got married or anything like that, because money is such a nice thing to have. And I know, Rollie, that you'd hate for me not to have what they call security.

"So I really don't see what I can do about these financial reverses, do you, Rollie? Really? So I'll just keep on expecting to get the nice checks every month, and while we're on the subject, the last one was almost two weeks late and I was almost worried, Rollie.

"But I wasn't really worried, Rollie. Because I know how sweet you are about things like that and also my lawyer says you haven't got a leg to stand on and that if we had to go to court he doesn't see how I could avoid bringing up all those playful little habits of yours which I'd simply hate to mention, Rollie, and didn't at the hearing because you were so sweet about the money.

"As ever,
"Peg-of-your-heart

"*Mr. Roland Fielding,*
Croton-on-Hudson,
New York"

Heimrich folded the carbon and passed it back to Forniss, who put it in his pocket and said, "Peg of his checkbook's more like it."

"Yes," Heimrich said. "The termite type."

"I heard the other day," Forniss said, "that down in Key West, where they've got lots of termites, they put tents over whole houses and run gas in and—poof, no more termites. No more anything."

"What will they think of next?" Heimrich said, and finished his coffee. He said, "We wouldn't want to keep Mr. Fielding from church or anything, Charlie. Even if he was up late last night. You've had it copied?" Forniss nodded. "I'll use the copy, then," Heimrich said.

Fielding, assuming the accuracy of a butler's report, assuming the man who had answered the telephone was a butler, had been in New York the night before, at the theater, and had not been expected home until late. They had decided not to wait up for him.

Forniss drove the car south, through Peekskill, along the Post Road. They did not hurry. It was unlikely that Mr. Fielding would be going anywhere. Fielding had a fine stone house near Croton-on-Hudson; a large house, reached by a winding drive. "He could use a few yards of gravel on this," Forniss said, as they drove up toward the house. "That big maple could have stood pruning last spring."

A man in a black coat answered the door. Mr. Fielding was just having breakfast. He didn't know whether—

"I think he'll want to see us," Heimrich said, and said, also, who they were. "When he's finished his breakfast," Heimrich said, and the man in the black coat said, doubtfully, "Well, I'll see," and let them in and gestured toward a large room—a comfortably furnished living room. There was a chessboard on a table, with a game partly played. They waited briefly in the large room. A big man came in through a doorway at the end of it—a big, loose man.

He was tall; he was partly bald; he had gray stubble on his cheeks and chin; he bulged somewhat above and below the belt of his slacks. He wore a pair of rimless bifocals and carried the news section of the *Daily News*. The headline of the *Daily News* could be read across the room. It said, "Peggy Belford Slain!" Under that it said, "Former Husband Kills Famed Actress and Self!"

The big, loose man said, "You get up early, gentlemen," in a husky voice. He said, "Might give a man time to shave." He came on into the room. "Have to admit I was expecting you," he said. "Which of you's Heimrich?"

Heimrich told him.

"On the other hand," Roland Fielding said, "says in the paper this man"—he turned over the front page of the *News* and looked at the third page—"Collins it is, killed her. So I was married to her a while back. So what?"

But the words were more truculent than the tone.

"Anyway," Fielding said, "sit down. I was out on the town last night. Getting too old for it, maybe."

He sat heavily. Heimrich sat. Forniss continued to stand and, for so large a man, became curiously inconspicuous. Which is part of his job.

"Now?" Fielding said.

Heimrich did the bit about routine.

"Specifically," he said, and handed the loose man the copy of the carbon copy. Fielding looked at it, read it. He looked at Heimrich with doubt. "Copy of a carbon copy," Heimrich said. "You got the letter?"

"Yes," Fielding said. "The gold-digging little bitch."

"You wanted to reduce her alimony?"

"Captain," Fielding said, "twenty-four thousand dollars a year is a lot of money. Also, she made a lot of money when she was working, and she worked a lot."

"She says financial reverses," Heimrich said.

"A man wants to save money," Fielding said. "Wants a little less gold digging. He says a lot of things." He held out the copy to Heimrich, who took it. "If you mean, could I go on paying her off—sure. Did I want to? I sure as hell didn't. So—" He shrugged his heavy shoulders, which was evidently a task. "I had a try. Result—that." He indicated the copy of the letter.

"These—playful little habits she writes about?"

"I don't know what the hell she was talking about," Fielding said. "Only, she'd tell any lies she figured there was money in." He got up heavily and walked heavily to a table and took a fat cigar out of a box. He lighted the cigar and went back and sat down. "I don't know what lies," he said.

"From this," Heimrich said, "I gather she had you—sewed up."

"Unless she married," Fielding said. "Or, of course, I could get the alimony order modified."

"In which case she would have told these—lies? In court, at the hearing?"

"What she said," Fielding told him. "I wouldn't put it past her. Or anything else, come to that."

"You've no idea what lies?"

"Captain," Fielding said, "Peggy had a thoroughly nasty little mind. How do I know? Whatever she thought would make the nastiest stink. Do me the most damage. Louse things up the most for me."

Heimrich waited.

"Captain," Fielding said, "I've got a lot of irons in the fire. Have to get along with all kinds of people. Some of them are pretty persnickety. See what I mean? No reason they should realize she was lying. I mean, if she lied in court. And—some of them wouldn't care a lot whether she was lying or not. Figure that just charging things did the damage."

"And—shy off?"

"Sure," Fielding said. "I've got a deal on now—" He stopped. "Never mind about that."

"Mr. Fielding," Heimrich said, "when you agreed to this very considerable alimony, I gather—"

"She was a headache," Fielding said. "A hell of a headache. O.K., I was a damn fool not to realize she would be before I got—hooked into it. But—well, you've seen her, captain. Any man—"

He did not finish. He did not particularly need to.

"What I was going to say," Heimrich told him, "was that when you agreed to this two thousand a month it wasn't as much of—well, call it a drain, as it's become recently?"

"Any time," Fielding said, "it's a lot of money. You're still on this 'financial reverses' thing? Forget it. Also, it was Collins killed her. Not me." He looked at Heimrich intently. "Didn't he kill her?"

"Apparently," Heimrich said. "We've got to check all angles, Mr. Fielding. Part of the job. For example—I suppose you were in New York yesterday afternoon? At your office?"

"Sure," Fielding said. "I—" And he stopped. "No," he said, "I drove up to see a man in Cold Harbor. Name of Goodman. Jacob Goodman. A man I've a deal going with. Didn't go anywhere near this Collins place, wherever it is."

"Now Mr. Fielding," Heimrich said. "I didn't suggest you had."

"Look," Fielding said, "you going to let the newspapers have that letter?"

"No."

"But you're going to hang on to it yourself?"

"For the moment," Heimrich said, "naturally, Mr. Fielding. Anything you want to ask, sergeant?"

Which was a signal.

Forniss said, "Nope. Guess not, captain," and they left, and left the loose man with an expression of relief on his unshaven face. Or so, at any rate, Heimrich thought. Facial expressions are not always so easily classified.

"This drive could sure as hell do with a few yards of gravel," Forniss said, as they drove down it. Heimrich agreed.

"The trim on the house could do with paint," Forniss said.

"I noticed, Charlie."

"Twenty-four thousand is a hell of a lot more than most people make in a year," Charles Forniss said, and turned onto the blacktop.

"Yes."

"What playful little habits?"

"Now Charlie," Heimrich said. "Surely your mind is as inventive as mine."

VII

THE TIME CLOCK which lives in the mind remembered that the day was Sunday, that there was no fabric shop to open on Van Brunt Avenue at ten o'clock. (Fabrics, Susan Faye has discovered, are not bought early, like groceries.) It was almost nine before the time clock in Susan's mind buzzed its notice and Susan wakened, and stretched and discovered that this was going to be really a hot one. A sticky hot one, a damp and misty hot one. The kind of day to be spent in the shade, or in a shaded pool.

Pool was the controlling word, of course. With that thought, with the picture of Brian Collins's pool, so artfully indoors yet so adaptable to the out-of-doors, the nagging returned to her mind—the sense that something was wrong with something. It was the thing which had for so long kept her half awake, her mind reeling through colored dreams until—

Damn it, Susan thought and swung long legs and slim body off the bed. Until what?

Because, there had been something. Something that, in dream, seemed to provide an explanation, an answer to nagging question. Something in her mind had said, at some period, "That's it," and the nagging had stopped, as a headache stops with enough aspirin. And now all she could think of was that this had, somehow, been connected with Colonel. Which, palpably, was absurd.

With no small boy to feed, there was not much sense in breakfast. Colonel appeared in the doorway of the bedroom and woofed, explaining that there was a great deal of sense in his. She fed the great dog, who finished in half a dozen gigantic gulps and turned his face up to her and looked wistful, a dog starved. Susan, in shorts and

[89]

shirt, made herself coffee and toast and thought of eggs and rejected them, and went out onto the terrace with toast and coffee, and with her mind nagging furiously.

It was a great deal worse now than it had been the night before, when she had so resolutely put her mind to it. Now she had had it and let it get away, which was infuriating. It was a dream, Susan told herself—just a dream, in which only dreams are solved. And what possibly could Colonel have had to do with it? Colonel came out, tongue hanging, and flopped in the shade, with the air of a dog who has just completed a hard day's work. After a few seconds of quiet, he snorted.

"Go—" Susan began, and realized that that was where Colonel had come into it; a snort, an injunction to go to sleep. After which she had gone to sleep herself—gone to sleep with the consciousness of something solved. Colonel had wakened her from half sleep by snorting and—

No, that wasn't it. She had wakened herself by talking in her sleep; the sound of her own voice had wakened her. And, in half wakefulness, she had been dimly surprised that she had heard not only her own voice, but the words she had used. Had, then, the feeling of something accomplished, something solved, resulted from whatever it was she had said, aloud, in sleep?

She told herself to skip it. She told herself that if she left it alone it would not go away, but would come back. Quit trying to remember and it jumps into the mind.

Finish your coffee. (Finished.) Light a cigarette. (Lighted.) Lie back and make the mind blank. (Blank; full of irritation.) You said something and waked yourself up and Colonel snorted—presumably in answer—and you told him to go to sleep and—"bad color." My God, Susan thought, sitting upright, my-God-it-worked! Now she had only to remember what she had meant by it. Bad color of what? Or, of whom?

Of, it was uglily possible, the dead. Of, it was certainly true, blood. She had dreamed red all night until she had—what? Decided that red was a bad color? That was absurd. Colors are not bad, or good. Except—except in relationship to one another, this color wrong with that color. (And even that, nine times out of ten, was untrue; was something which people who did not really see colors had been taught, had taught themselves, to see.) Red is, of course, a little tricky; red is a noisy color, a bully of a color. A "wrong" color, sometimes. And what, my girl, has that got to do with anything, and don't now—it's daylight now—fill your mind with that picture in which the red is blood.

And Merton—how could I ever have thought of calling him Ricky?—is perfectly capable of solving whatever there is (if anything) to solve without my having notions. Without, for heaven's sake, a woman's intuition. If—

It was in his studio. That's where there was something wrong about it; something that jarred, that was wrong in the picture. And, I won't be able to think of anything else until I know what it was. So the thing to do—

The Inn thought Captain Heimrich had gone out, and Sergeant Forniss with him. The Inn would check. The Inn did check. Both gone, whereabouts unknown. So she could not ask him if, assuming she drove over to the Collins house, she would be able to get into it, and go to the studio and see if she could find, again, what was wrong in it. She put the telephone receiver back. The thing to do was to forget the whole business, and do around the house those things which were always waiting to be done. So—

So Susan Faye put on a linen dress instead of shorts and shirt (since it was, after all, Sunday) and got into her car and drove toward the hilltop house of the late Brian Collins. If she couldn't get in, she couldn't get in, and no harm done, and it was somewhat cooler driving. If she could get in, she would look around the studio

—nobody had died in the studio; shed blood there—and find it or not find it.

Colonel, drooling slightly and looking as pleased as it was in his face to look—his sin, whatever it was, had apparently been forgiven —rode on the seat beside her. Seated so, he was considerably taller than Susan. Now and then he put his head out the window for the breeze. Susan drove up Sugar Creek Lane to its abrupt ending and started up the narrow, hilly drive (lane, really) to the glass and redwood house. She had gone up it about two hundred yards and was just starting around one of its corners when a horn sounded warning. Susan sounded back, and stopped. The car coming down slowed. It was a Buick station wagon, driven by a man—a tall man. That much Susan noticed; then, as the Buick stopped, sunlight reflected from its windshield, and she could no longer see the driver.

Not that it mattered. Susan's was, as the upbound car, obviously "it." She backed down the hill again, backed slowly and with care. The Buick edged down after her. At the road again, she backed toward the road's ending, toward the sign which said, so advisedly, "Stop." The Buick reached the driveway's end, turned sharply to the left down Sugar Creek Lane, and hooted its thanks. Colonel, for reasons of his own, leaned out and barked at it. Susan turned back into the driveway and went up it, with no great confidence. For all she knew, there might be half a dozen cars up there, all planning to come down.

There was only one car on the turnaround—a state police car. It was empty. After a moment a young trooper came around the house and up to Susan's car.

Colonel pricked up his ears; he made a soft bleating sound, as if he were trying to purr. He made movements, as if to get out of the car. He had, after too long a time, met again one of his chosen. "Hi-yah?" the trooper said, to Colonel, and reached in and scratched behind one of the large ears. He spoke more formally to Susan Faye. He said, "Morning, Mrs. Faye. The captain isn't here."

(It occurred to Susan, briefly, that Merton Heimrich himself apparently was the only person who did not make the connection.)

"Oh," she said. "Mr. Crowley. I didn't think he would be. Is it all right for me to go in?"

"Why," Raymond Crowley said. "Sure, I guess so, Mrs. Faye. I don't see why not."

And, Susan thought, wondered why. It seemed rather a long, vague thing to go into.

"Mr. Collins," she said, "did a design he wanted me to look at. Yesterday—you know I was with the captain when—when we found them?"

Crowley did. He said it was a bad thing to walk in on.

"I only glanced at what Mr. Collins had done," she said. "The design. Is it all right if I go look at it again?"

It was of course all right. Unless she wanted him, however, Trooper Crowley would not go in with her. She knew her way. Also, any time now, the reporters and photographers could be expected. The captain had promised them they could look at the house, inside and out; take what pictures they wanted. Crowley unlocked the glass door.

There was nothing to show where the blood had been. The chair Collins had died in had been removed. (Which would, Susan suspected, disappoint the press.) There was a chalk outline to show where the girl had lain. Susan went along the corridor to the studio. It was as it had been the evening before, except that now the light was much better. Brian Collins must, she thought, have done most of his work in the morning.

The nude portrait of Peggy Belford was still on the easel, but covered. At least, she supposed it was the same, and lifted enough of the shrouding canvas to make sure it was. But the "wrong" thing didn't, she was sure, lie in the nude. She had looked at it carefully; if what she sought was here, it was something she had glanced at quickly, seen with half her mind. What else had they done here?

He, of course, had looked for, and found, the design. He had turned several canvases toward her and she had glanced at them, not bothering to see them, until prompted, he had looked for, found the right thing. Had there been something wrong about one of the canvases? And, if there had, could it have any possible bearing? She stood and looked around and shook her head, all expectation draining out of her mind. A chase of the wild goose, obviously. A search for will-o'-the-wisp. She should have stayed home and washed stockings. Customers of fabric shops expect young women running them to wear stockings.

Unless— She moved canvases on stretchers; found the design that yesterday—and how long ago that seemed!—she had come to look at. She moved it out into the light and propped it on a chair, facing the light, and moved away from it. And red jumped out at her.

The less adequate light of the evening before, her own preoccupation with things most hideously immediate, explained it—had to explain it. But even making those allowances, it was difficult to see why she had not at once remembered the red that jumped from Brian Collins's free-form design. The red so utterly "wrong"; so glaringly, insolently, bullying the muted tones among which it was supposed to live. A red so wrong that it was—why, it was almost a joke!

What on earth had come over Brian Collins? Sudden color-blindness? Or had it all been planned as a meaningless, rather cruel, joke on her—on a person he barely knew?

She turned others of the paintings which were stacked against the wall, reassuring herself about Brian Collins. He had been a painter; he had seen color. She did not like all the canvases—the several canvases—she glanced at, but that meant nothing, except that some of them she did not like. In all of them, he had been a painter.

Had somebody else daubed red, "wrong" red, on the design as a kind of sabotage? Peggy Belford? With only the intention to annoy? It was hard to believe; it was impossible to believe, to explain on what she knew. Or—someone else? Someone unknown, for reasons unguessable?

She put the canvases back where she had found them. I've run out of guesses, she thought. She looked at the design again, and again red leaped at her eyes, clawing. There could be no doubt that it was "wrong." Anybody not blind would know it wrong. She looked more closely, trying to decide whether the red patches—there were three of them—had been painted, daubed on, more recently than the other colors. She could not be sure; she doubted whether anybody could be sure. He had used gouache, which dries quickly, which is opaque.

She was suddenly sure of one thing. Brian Collins had not used this color, if it was he who had used it, by accident. If he had used it it was for some purpose. To—red is the color of blood. *It is also the color of danger!*

She heard voices; a good many voices. They came from the main part of the house. That would be, she decided, the press.

They didn't, she thought, know that she had been with Heimrich when he found the bodies. At least, she hoped they didn't, because if they did they would want what they called an "eyewitness." A role she had no desire to play.

There was a door in the studio which led out to the garden. She remembered that; found that; went out through that. The turnaround in front of the house, when she went around the house to it, was crowded with half a dozen cars. A number of men were in the house, to be seen through the glass wall. Flashlight bulbs were going off briskly. Her car, probably, would be blocked off and—

It was not. Trooper Raymond Crowley evidently had seen to that.

She took the way out, crept down the long, precipitous driveway and did not encounter anybody coming up it. She turned down Sugar Creek Lane, driving slowly, her mind puzzled. She had found out one thing; there could be no doubt of that. But what she had found out seemed only to make things dimmer.

She went around a corner, and the rear of another car was disappearing around the next corner. A wagon. The Buick? No, that was absurd. The Buick would be miles away, by now. Another Buick wagon, obviously.

"Woof," Colonel said, casually, from the seat beside her.

***

Heimrich was asked if he had ever tried to get reaction out of a piece of putty. He was told that that was what it came to, always came to.

The man who asked, without expecting an answer, who told what it always had come to, was dark and wiry and violent—violent in quick movements of hands and body, in explosive voice. A wedge of black hair jutted down his forehead; the hair bristled like the fur on the spine of an angry cat. The man strode back and forth across what the Cold Harbor Motor Lodge likes to think of as "the patio." Anton Zersk was staying at the Cold Harbor Motor Lodge because he got enough of actors on the set. This was one of the first things he told Heimrich, at a little before eleven on Sunday morning. The next thing he told him was that if they could get one—just *one*—morning without this haze—this *damn* haze—they could finish up and pack up and get the hell out of there.

He told Heimrich also, in bursts, that he hadn't had the faintest idea that Brian Collins was in Van Brunt Center the day before, since he hadn't been there himself; that he had heard Peggy Belford say something about going to Collins's for a swim and that he hadn't cared where she went as long as she was, even briefly, out of his hair. He hit his bristling hair angrily, to show what he meant, or to brush vestiges of Peggy Belford's past occupancy out of it. He said he was damn sorry about Collins, who was too good a man to throw himself away on anything like Peggy Belford.

"You knew him?" Heimrich said.

"Not him," Zersk said. "His stuff. Some of it was damn good stuff. And for that little bitch he shoots himself. For *that!*" Zersk managed, somehow, to make "that" a harsher epithet than the other. Then he stopped in his pacing. "Or didn't he?" Zersk asked.

"Everything indicates he did," Heimrich said, mildly. "We're more or less picking up the pieces, Mr. Zersk. See that there isn't anything left over. You didn't like Miss Belford, evidently."

Zersk sat down suddenly. He did everything suddenly. He had bounced out of his room suddenly when Heimrich knocked on the door, asked to talk to him.

Now he said that Peggy Belford had been a pain, and said where. And was asked why.

"Unscrupulous little gold digger, for one thing," Zersk said. "And don't look so damn hopeful. She didn't dig me. Because there isn't any gold for one thing, and she knew I was on to her for another. So?"

"I'm not," Heimrich said, even more mildly than before, "accusing you, or anybody else, of anything. You objected to her lack of scruple?"

Then Zersk laughed. He laughed explosively, also.

"Heimrich," he said, "I had to direct her. Otherwise, I didn't give a damn what she was. She could make a million or drop dead. Anything, so long as I didn't have to try to get a performance out of a wooden Indian. Or a piece of putty. You ever try to get a reaction out of a piece of putty?"

Heimrich said he hadn't.

"This one's the third time," Zersk said. "Three times—*three* times.

Yelling at her, pleading with her, saying, 'Nice Peggy, pretty Peggy. Listen Peggy. You loved this man. This man is dead, Peggy. D-e-a-d. You're sorry, sweetheart. You're all broken up, darling. You loved him and now he's dead and you haven't got anything more to live for. All right, lover, if that's too hard—that stinking little pooch of yours has been run over and he's dying and he looks up at you with those idiotic goddamn eyes and you're sorry, baby. Just think about the poor, dying little pooch—'" He broke off. "So," he said, "she pouts, like always. And, I give you my word, the pooch did get run over and you know what she actually did? She pouted. Just like always."

"But," Heimrich said, "you seem to have kept on giving her parts."

Zersk leaped out of the chair. For a moment, it appeared that he was about to leap at Heimrich. Instead, he shouted at Heimrich.

"*Me?*" he shouted. "*I* gave her parts?"

"Somebody. Not you?"

"Listen, Heimrich. They hire me to direct. They say here's the usual corny script and here's the half-witted actors and you've got so many weeks for this and so many for that and we expect a masterpiece or anyway a few million dollars' profit." He stopped suddenly. "All right," he said. "Take part of it back. Frank Dale's a hell of a good actor and George Latham's learning to do what he's told. And the script's no worse than most. I'll get a picture out of it and—Paul Marley hired her. It's the third time he's hired her. No—fourth. One of them Micky Fowler got stuck with."

"All right," Heimrich said. "Why? If she was as bad as you say."

"Shape," Zersk said. "Men drooled. And women—I guess women put it up to their husbands. 'See what a decent dress will do for a girl? Buy me a decent dress, you no-count.' Thinking they'd look like Peggy if they had the clothes Peggy always got in the last reel. No, last but one, usually. So, box office. That enough explanation?"

"Is there more?"

"Only," Zersk said, "that Paul's had a thing for her for years. Even before Gertrude died." He stopped. "There was a woman could act," he said. "God how she could act."

"Miss Belford didn't—respond?"

"Miss Belford," Zersk said, "was the marrying kind. Married where it would do the most good. My guess is that she was cold as a fish."

Heimrich raised his eyebrows.

"If you mean by that, did I try?" Zersk said. "No, I never tried. I've been married ten years—make it almost eleven—to a real live woman. Put on a few pounds after the first kid and maybe a few more after the girl came, and she's a real live woman, and when she's unhappy she cries and when she's happy she laughs and if anybody ever suggested she ought to be an actress she'd laugh like hell."

He looked at Heimrich rather balefully.

"I see," Heimrich said. "But Mr. Marley couldn't marry Miss Belford, since he was already married. So?"

"Casting her? I don't know. Maybe he didn't give up. Maybe he figured he'd keep her sweetened up on the chance things might—change. She was pretty sure to come unmarried at intervals. And—well, Gertrude was a good deal older than Paul." He got up and began to walk back and forth on the grass of "the patio." He said, "I sound like a heel all at once. Paul's a good enough guy. And, except for this Peggyitis, a pretty good producer. An all-right man to work with."

"Mr. Zersk," Heimrich said, "Mrs. Marley died about eighteen months ago, I understand. Some months before Miss Belford divorced Fielding?"

"Fielding?" Zersk repeated. "Oh—that outside guy. Automobiles or something, wasn't it?"

"Various things, I gather," Heimrich said.

"As to the time—I don't remember exactly. Ask Louella. Or, I suppose it was in the papers. Gertrude's overdose sure as hell was." He shook his head. "The damnedest thing," he said. "Why the hell did she?"

Heimrich made no suggestions, assuming none to have been requested.

Zersk sat down again. He sat down with as much vigor as most men jump.

"From what I hear," Zersk said. "From what she said, as a matter of fact, Belford was getting very nice alimony from this—" Apparently he had difficulty remembering the name of this outsider. He snapped his fingers. "Fielding. Mostly, alimony stops when a woman gets married again." He looked at Heimrich.

"Apparently," Heimrich said, "it would have this time."

"Of course," Zersk said, "it also stops when the woman dies."

"Now Mr. Zersk," Heimrich said. "Naturally. I take it that Mr. Marley hasn't a great deal of money?"

"He makes plenty," Zersk said. "Of course it's damn hard to hold on to—" And stopped. And looked at Heimrich with dark intensity. He said, "Why?" explosively.

All he meant, Heimrich said, was that Marley had not had enough money to tempt Peggy Belford to sacrifice the very nice alimony she was getting from Fielding. He assumed that that had been in Mr. Zersk's mind. Granting his estimate of Peggy Belford, of what Peggy Belford had been after.

Zersk said, "Oh." Then he said, "The kid got it," and seemed to think he had explained things. Heimrich shook his head.

"Gertrude had a lot," Zersk said. "Had saved plenty—you could put it away when she was making it, and she did. And old Waggoner left her plenty more. But it all went to the kid." He paused; made the explanation complete. "Chris," he said. "Her daughter."

"Nothing to Marley?"

That was what Zersk heard. Heimrich could always ask Marley himself. It didn't seem to Zersk that that was so surprising; Marley was making plenty. Didn't need more. The girl—well, it was natural for a mother to want her daughter to have everything she needed, if it ran to that.

"She's underage, isn't she?" Heimrich said. "Probably has a guardian. Marley?"

Anton Zersk said that Chris was a baby and considered, and said he thought just over seventeen. He didn't know anything about a guardian. When he spoke of Chris Waggoner, Zersk's barbed voice was less barbed. He even smiled faintly; Heimrich though unconsciously.

"She seems a nice child," Heimrich said, testing.

"Very," Zersk said. "All full of nonsense, like a lot of nice kids are. You should see her do her queen of tragedy bit."

"I did," Heimrich said. "Guess I did. She wants to be an actress?"

Zersk said, "Why sure," as if the question were absurd. "Will be, too, if she gets the breaks. She's another live one—going to be, anyhow. Already been badgering Marley to give her bits. Only, of course, she doesn't think about bits. Leads. For example, she thought she would be a lot better than Peggy in this opus."

"Would she have?"

"Well," Zersk said. "You mean in the box office? No. Not yet. You mean doing the part? Who wouldn't?"

"Actually? Or just because—"

"Peggy got in my hair? So I'm not objective? You've got something there, of course. All the same—yes, with no training—she's had a few months at an acting school and we'll have to knock that out of her—still, she'd have been better. With a choke collar and me at the other end of the lead."

"She was jealous of Miss Belford?"

Zersk was up and walking. He walked over to Heimrich and glared at him. He said, "Why?" and made it an expletive. Heimrich closed his eyes; after a second or two opened them and said, "Now Mr. Zersk. Because Miss Belford had a part she wanted. Wasn't that what we were talking about?"

Zersk continued to glare at him.

"Or," Heimrich said, "because the girl had a crush on Mr. Dale and Mr. Dale was paying attention to Miss Belford to discourage Miss Waggoner?"

"Who says that?" Zersk demanded.

"Oh," Heimrich said. "Mr. Dale."

He stood up then and thanked Anton Zersk and said Mr. Zersk had been helpful and that he appreciated it. And left, and could feel Zersk glaring at him as he walked to his car. A very intense man, Mr. Zersk, and one who had given him several things to think about.

He thought about them driving back to the Old Stone Inn, where Forniss awaited him, with one or two more things for them to think about. Item: Roland Fielding had driven up to Cold Harbor the afternoon before and had talked to one Jacob Goodman about a deal. And that had been at around two o'clock and the conference had taken about half an hour. And it is a twenty-minute drive from Cold Harbor to the Van Brunt area. Item: It was difficult to get much on Sunday, but Forniss had remembered a man he knew in New York. (Heimrich is always a little surprised at the variety of men Forniss knows, and the variety of places he knows them in.) This man said that Roland Fielding did, indeed, have a number of irons in a number of fires—the export of new and used cars, primarily to South America, was one of the irons—and that there were rumors around that some of the fires had cooled off in the last year or so. Nothing too definite; something to think about.

"Twenty-four grand is twenty-four grand," Forniss said. "He could have got to the Collins place in plenty of time."

"Expecting to find Miss Belford there? Alone? Knowing that Collins was going to come into town for his pictures?"

"She could have told him," Forniss said. "Or somebody else could. He could have seen Collins here. Or somebody could have told him Collins was here. Or—I can think of half a dozen more. He could have asked here at the Inn and somebody—"

"I know," Heimrich said. "Anything else?"

George Latham, the juvenile lead, wasn't around, and nobody seemed to know where he was. "Could be," Forniss said, "he's gone to church. Ought to be back pretty soon if he has." It was then a little after noon. "And," Forniss said, "Mrs. Faye called. Wonders if you can call back or stop by."

Heimrich looked pleased, and was not conscious of it. Sergeant Forniss did not mention this, by word or expression. Heimrich said, very casually, "All right, Charlie" and then, "Who do you know in L.A., Charlie? Hollywood?"

"Well," Forniss said, "there's Ben Cohen. On one of the papers. Nice guy. Saved my life once on one of those damn beaches. Makes him feel obligated. And a guy named Cooke, who's on the cops in L.A. And a second cousin of mine who's a cameraman at—"

"All right," Heimrich said. "Call the gossipiest, Charlie. And the one who might know the most. Pick up what you can. About all of them. And about Mrs. Waggoner, who died about a year ago and seems to have left her money, and she seems to have had money, to her daughter. Wheat and chaff, Charlie."

"Yep," Charles Forniss said.

"And, of course, whether Dale appeared to be as—call it casual—about Miss Belford as he indicates. And whether Anton Zersk is as happily married as—" He stopped. He said, "Sorry, Charlie."

"O.K.," Forniss said. "I'll call Ben. From the barracks."

"Naturally, Charlie," Captain Heimrich said.

VIII

THERE IS NO use using a telephone when, with ten minutes of driving, one can talk face to face. Heimrich told himself that, driving up Van Brunt Avenue, turning left, and toward the Hudson, on High Road. He found it entirely convincing. Turning into the driveway between the boulders, he found he had overestimated the time needed. Eight minutes.

Susan wore a sleeveless white tennis dress; its pleated skirt swirled around brown legs as she walked toward him across the terrace. How, Heimrich thought, could he ever have thought she wasn't pretty, but only fun to look at? Pretty? Make it beautiful.

"If you haven't eaten," Susan Faye said, "it gives sandwiches, Merton."

It was, she thought, as good a time as any other to get that established.

Heimrich was somewhat relieved, but at the same time—ridiculously—disappointed. He wasn't the Ricky type. That went without saying. He was the Merton type. Which probably, also, went without saying. "I could use a sandwich," Heimrich said, and let himself touch the nearest of the slender brown arms as they crossed the terrace to a table, to chairs at it, to a place with a napkin over it. It was surprising how cool the brown arm was under his fingers, considering how hot the day was, how muggy.

"Fill the glasses," she told him. "I'll get the coffee."

He filled tall glasses with as much ice from the bucket as they would hold. She came back—how could she look so fresh on such a drippy day?—with a glass coffee maker shaped like an hourglass and poured steaming coffee on ice.

"Now," Susan Faye said, "I remembered something, half remembered something. I couldn't get in touch with you so I went up to the house to see."

"Susan," Heimrich said, "I don't want you taking—"

"Sh-h-h," Susan said. "Listen. Anyway, Ray Crowley was there. And, before I left, the house bulged with reporters. Now, listen."

He listened. He did not ask whether she was sure the color was "wrong." He would as soon have asked an expert from the Fingerprint Bureau if he was sure this print matched that print. She finished and waited, eating a sandwich, sipping iced coffee.

"You think," Heimrich said, "that somebody put this glaring red on over the original color? As a message?" She nodded. He closed his eyes for a moment. "I'd think," he said, "that the original color would show through. I mean—influence the color added. Bleed through it."

"No," she said. "We use gouache for this sort of thing. That or show card colors. But this was gouache. It comes in tubes and—" She paused. "Anyway," she said, "it's opaque. That's the point. Water colors run. Gouache covers completely. Nothing shows through it."

Heimrich nodded. It was, he said, a somewhat obscure message. Of course, Collins had known that Susan was coming. Been confident she would notice.

She supposed so.

"But," she said, "then put it against the wall? Where I wouldn't see it unless I looked? He probably worked on it on the easel. Why not leave it there? Instead of putting this nude of the girl there." She stopped. "You see what it comes to?" she said.

"Now Susan," Heimrich began, and smiled suddenly. "Yes, Susan," he said. "I see what it comes to. There was somebody else there. Somebody Collins had reason to fear. Probably, somebody who was holding a gun on him."

"And set the stage," she said. "Rather—stagily. Why?"

"Oh," Heimrich said. "There was a time lag to be accounted for. At least, that seems most likely. Collins died some time after the girl. A good many people think a doctor can look at a body and say, 'Died two hours and fifteen minutes ago.' Which a doctor can't. But, the time difference was there and our somebody wanted to account for it, figuring nobody would believe a man would merely sit for a couple of hours and look at a woman he'd killed."

"That," Susan said, "is about as easy for me to believe as—as this other. His getting out the picture and arranging her body and all the rest of it."

"Yes," Heimrich said. "For you. For me. But in plays, movies, people don't merely sit and—brood. They do things, or say things. 'To be or not to be.' I suspect that people in the profession get to—well, supposing that all things move at that tempo."

What he was saying, Susan told him, was that one of the people in the movie company had been the somebody. Of course, that was something which leaped to the mind. She paused. "Too quickly?" she said and Heimrich nodded his head, pleased with her, and said, "Perhaps." One learned to be suspicious of ideas that jumped into the mind, suspecting they had been nudged to jump. He told her briefly of Marley and of Zersk, of the pretty histrionic Chris; he told her about the loose man named Roland Fielding.

"Somehow," Susan said, "he doesn't sound that bright. I mean if this was staged so that, first, it would look like Brian and then, if that fell through, like someone who thinks in theatrical terms—" There was doubt in her voice.

"He plays chess," Heimrich said. "I don't know how well, of course. At least, there was a chessboard, set up, in his living room. In chess, one thinks some moves ahead."

"I," Susan said, "was never any good even at checkers. Look, darling—"

He did look. There was that to be said. And then, apparently, he decided merely that her tongue had slipped, or that, talking of people of the theater, she had fallen momentarily into the phraseology of the theater. There was that to be observed.

"Merton," she said. "Does this really prove anything? Or, is there some other explanation? That Brian was only trying something that didn't come off?"

She was asked if she thought that. She shook her head.

She had had it in her mind longer than he had. Had she another explanation? Sudden color-blindness she rejected. Then?

"Somebody else might have done it," she said, with doubt. "Any of those who had been there. Any time yesterday."

"My dear," Heimrich said, "if we're going to include somebody else— Peggy herself. Why? Malicious mischief, like drawing of mustaches on girls on posters?"

It was possible, Susan pointed out, and was told that, always, there were a great many possibilities; that, always, almost anything was possible. And that Peggy Belford did not seem to have been a young woman to indulge in pranks which got her nowhere. She was a young woman who kept carbon copies of her letters; who added with precision and subtracted with reluctance. Or, seemed to have been. Of course, it was possible that, stepping out of character, she had daubed at Collins's design and, being caught at it, had been killed for her desecration.

"Merton!" Susan said.

He pointed out that, as she had suggested, anything is possible. One chooses among possibilities.

"You said, 'Prove anything,'" Heimrich said. "Against the obvious physical evidence, in court, no, probably not. But—it's something that would have to be explained away. By a defense attorney, if we turn up somebody who needs defending. Up till now there hasn't been. So— State's Exhibit A, if it ever comes to that."

"Will it?"

"My dear," Heimrich said, "I begin to think it may." He finished the last of his coffee. "You'd better come along," he said. "Pick up the exhibit."

She started to say something; started to say, "To help you carry it?" and caught herself. Because there was no reason to disturb a pleasant balance, when he was so difficult a man to bring into balance.

"To help me carry it," Merton Heimrich said gravely, to the astonishment of Susan Faye.

They were on Sugar Creek Lane, almost at the turnoff to the Collins house, when Susan said there was one thing she had forgotten to tell him, and told him about the station wagon which had come down as she was going up.

"One of them picking up the car," Heimrich said. "The one Miss Belford drove up in. I told Marley it would be all right and passed the word along to Crowley. I suppose it was Marley himself?"

She didn't know. A man, half hidden seen behind a glary windshield. And she had had enough to look at, in the mirror, then craned out the window, as she backed down.

They went, cautiously, up the narrow, curving driveway. There was no police car in the turnaround. "Told him to lock up after the press finished," Heimrich said, swinging the car around to face again toward the driveway. "Other things for him to do, once he'd seen the reporters didn't carry away souvenirs and—" He stopped. He was looking at the open garage. There were again two cars in it—the jeep and, this time, an open Chevrolet. With a rental company's plate above its license plate. Which was—

They walked quickly across the terrace to the glass wall, the glass door. And stopped, and Susan drew her breath in quickly and, as quickly, Heimrich put steadying fingers on a brown arm.

Inside the room, in a chair near the fireplace, a man sat slumped. Nearer the fireplace, a girl lay on her back, on the floor, one knee drawn up so that the pose was one of grace. The girl wore a white bathing suit which molded her slender body. Dark hair swirled about her head. Neither man nor girl moved. Horribly, the man seemed lifeless in the chair.

And Susan, trembling a little, said, "*No!*" the word only a breath.

For a moment they stood, side by side, frozen. Then Heimrich moved quickly—moved two steps quickly toward the glass door. And the girl on the floor turned her head to look at him, and the man in the chair turned too. They watched for a moment as Heimrich opened the unlocked door and then Chris Waggoner got up off the floor, seemed to flow up off the floor. When Susan and Heimrich stood inside the house and looked at the two, Chris said, "Oh!" in a surprised, uneasy voice. And the man got up and faced them, and he smiled a little.

He was a tall young man in polo shirt and walking shorts; an uncommonly handsome young man, with thick, rather long, blond hair. His body tapered from broad shoulders to narrow hips. He was, at a guess, in his early twenties.

"Well?" Heimrich said, and then, "You were in the wrong place, Miss Waggoner. Miss Belford's body couldn't be seen from outside."

"I—I know," the girl said, in a girl's voice. "I just couldn't—couldn't bring myself to—" She stopped. When she resumed it was in the low voice, the voice with a throb in it. "We were re-enacting," she throbbed. "Seeking the—" She paused. "The inwardness," she said.

"I see," Merton Heimrich said. "Did you find it, Miss Waggoner?" His voice was very grave.

She looked at him, now with suspicion. There was nothing in his expression to confirm suspicion, or to allay it.

"One must live the part," she said, and still throbbed, but with, Heimrich thought, lessened confidence. "Re-creating the physical circumstances—" She stopped, confidence quite gone. "All right," Chris said. "No. This is Georgie-Por—this is George Latham, Captain Heimrich."

The handsome, tall young man said, "How-ja-do, captain? Was the posture right?"

"Approximately," Heimrich said. "I suppose you two read the newspaper accounts?"

They had.

"The police re-enact scenes," Chris said. "You know they do."

"Sometimes," Heimrich said. "With suspects. How did you get in here?"

"The door wasn't locked," Latham said. He had an easy, pleasant voice, an easy, pleasant manner. "Are we under arrest? For breaking and entering?" He did not seem noticeably disturbed by the possibility. He looked at Susan. He said, "Miss—?"

Susan told them; told them both. She also said, "If you two had seen it, you wouldn't feel so chipper. Also, that isn't the right chair, Mr. Latham."

"We've taken the right chair," Heimrich said. "What did you expect to prove? Either of you?"

"We expected—" the girl said, speaking as a girl, and paused to consider. "To *feel* something," she said, partly in the other voice.

"There is one thing," Latham said. "Did Peggy die—very quickly, captain? Or would she have had time—"

"To arrange things," Chris said. "To make herself look—graceful? Don't think that wouldn't have been the first thing in her mind. Even if she was dying she'd have—"

"Chris," Latham said. "Be your age."

It was, Heimrich thought, the injunction she would be least likely to relish. Apparently it was. Chris directed a glance at Latham; obviously a withering glance. Latham did not, however, perceptibly wither. "Baby," he said, with affection. With, Susan Faye thought, at least affection.

"Miss Belford was dead by the time she hit the floor," Heimrich said.

And then, as if for the first time she had realized that they talked of death, not of its mimicry on the stage, Chris Waggoner's pale face lost the glow under the skin and the color on her wide, sensitive mouth stood out, unreal against pallor. And Latham moved to her quickly and put an arm around her shoulders. For an instant, she let him; relaxed to him. But it was only for an instant and, although she said nothing, Latham took his arm from around her.

"Then," George Latham said, "somebody must have arranged the body. Collins? Because—I shot a deer once. Only once. It didn't fall —prettily."

"We had thought of that, Mr. Latham," Heimrich said, and the young man flushed. He managed to smile while the flush still held. "I suppose," he said, "we've been pretty silly. To think we could help."

"Now Mr. Latham," Heimrich said, and added that perhaps he could, and asked the usual questions. Latham had not, he said, known that Brian Collins had been in the village the afternoon before. He had known that Peggy Belford planned to go to the Collins house—"to come here"—for a swim. They had all known that. He had been in his room at the Inn, alone.

"I've got a scene coming up," he said. "When we get back to the Coast. Tony thinks I haven't quite got it yet, and I was going over it. In front of a mirror."

"All afternoon?"

"From the time we got back from location and had lunch until— Oh, I guess about six. When I got thirsty."

"I don't suppose," Heimrich said, "that you've any idea who might have wanted to kill Miss Belford? If, of course, Collins didn't?"

"Which means," Latham said, "you think he didn't?"

"Assuming," Heimrich said. "Just assuming, Mr. Latham."

"I wouldn't," Latham said, "say that Peggy was universally admired. If she—well, knew where anybody's buried a body— But—" He broke off; he looked at Chris Waggoner.

"So," she said, "you've come around to it," and turned to Heimrich. "If it wasn't Mr. Collins," she said, and spoke as a girl, but firmly, "she was blackmailing somebody. All you've got to do is find out who, captain. Whose body she knew about and—"

She stopped speaking very suddenly. And her widely spaced eyes widened; there was a fixed expression in her wide eyes.

"Yes?" Heimrich said, after they had waited a moment.

But she merely shook her head, slowly, but so that the heavy dark hair flowed with the head's movement. Then, after several seconds, she said, "Nothing," and now her various voices came to one—one flat voice, a voice without inflection.

"What have you thought of, Miss Waggoner?" Heimrich asked her, but again she shook her head and again, in the same flat tone, "Nothing. Nothing at all." The blankness remained in her dark eyes. It was as if they were focused on something very far away. Then she blinked, as if to blink back to the immediate and said, "George. I want to go."

She spoke like a girl—a girl a little over seventeen; an uneasy girl.

Latham looked at Heimrich, and Heimrich said, "Of course."

"Come on, baby," Latham said, gently, and in that moment seemed much older than the girl; much older, indeed, than he looked. "It was a fool thing to do," he added, to nobody in particular, seemingly in explanation of what they had done. They went. Outside the car started; it backed out of the garage—why had they put it in the garage? Heimrich wondered. Of course, it was the easiest place to put it—and turned and went down toward Sugar Creek Lane, Latham driving.

"She thought of something," Susan said, and Heimrich said, "Yes, Susan."

" 'Whose body she knew about' she said and then, thought of something."

"Yes," Heimrich said. "A very changeable girl, isn't she? Let's go look at this design, Susan. This wrong color."

They went along the corridor, into the studio. The nude on the easel had been uncovered. There were several used flashbulbs in a wastepaper basket. The photographers had been neat beyond their custom. "I'd think," Susan said, looking at the portrait of Peggy Belford, "that it would be a little explicit for newspaper reproduction. However—I put it back over there."

She went "over there." She pulled the drawing board out and turned it around. And they both looked, blankly, at an empty expanse of drawing board. The color-mottled paper was gone. In one corner, a strip of tape still held a corner of drawing paper.

"Somebody—" Susan said, staring at the board; at the revealing triangle of torn-off paper.

"Got here ahead of us," Heimrich said. "Yes." He looked away, around the room; looked at a big window in the side of the room—not the skylight; a window next to a narrow door. He turned back to Susan.

"Susan," he said, "when you were looking at it, seeing there was something wrong with it, do you suppose a person watching you could have realized you *did* see something wrong with it?"

He saw surprise; consideration, on her expressive face, and his question was, he thought, answered.

"Yes," she said, "I suppose so. I looked at it carefully, from different angles. Studied it. Anyone watching me would have seen that. And—I suppose that something about it puzzled me."

"When you left, you went back through the main part of the house?"

She told him about that; how she had avoided the reporters; pointed to the narrow door through which she had left the studio, told of going around the house to her car.

"Then—" he said, but did not finish that, and said, "Wait a minute," and went to the telephone on the table. He dialed and waited; he said, "Send out a call to Crowley. Send him here," and hung up and sat for a moment looking at the telephone. Then he looked down. A drawer in the table was partly open. He opened it farther and leaned down and Susan could see his nostrils move as he sniffed the inside of the drawer.

He looked up and nodded. "Oil," he said. "Probably where he kept the gun. Anybody could have found it, without much looking. Collins might have mentioned it, shown it, to anybody he trusted. Somebody could have said, 'Don't you get nervous up here so far from anybody else?' and he might have said, 'No, why should I? And, anyway, I've got a gun handy.'"

He stood up.

"Merton," she said. "Doesn't this prove—pretty much prove, that it wasn't Brian? Was somebody else? That Brian was trying to leave a message and that now somebody has—well, made off with the message? So that—"

She stopped suddenly.

"So that now you're the only one who can be sure there was a message," Heimrich said. "Can testify to what was wrong with the picture. The little flaw in the composition. It could be that way."

He looked again at the window. He went over and looked at the narrow door. The lock was of a familiar type—a plunger was set into the knob. Pressed by someone leaving, the plunger held and the door was locked. Unless, by intention or by accident, one turned the inner knob. When the knob was turned the plunger popped up, the door was no longer locked.

Susan thought she had locked the door when she went out; supposed she had; tried to remember clearly and ended by shaking her head. It was something one did, if one did it at all, without thinking about it, the action almost reflexive.

"Go out," Heimrich said. "This seems to be a day for re-enactment. Try not to think what you're doing. Think—oh, of the fact that the red was wrong. Wonder if it meant anything."

"That," Susan said, "is what our youthful friends would call The Method. At least, as I understand—"

She did not finish. She went to the door and opened it and stepped out onto a narrow, flagged walk. As her fingers left the inner knob, the index finger pressed the plunger. But—as her hand slid from the inner knob, moved to the knob outside, the inner knob turned slightly. Turned enough.

"Damn," Susan said, and reached back in.

"Never mind," Heimrich said. "Come back in. It's very easy to do. It's also pretty easy to lock one's self out, accidentally. The old types were—"

It was also a day for not finishing the obvious. Heimrich went outside and stood, among bushes, and looked in through the window, while Susan looked out at him. He looked down at the ground, bent down to examine, shrugged his shoulders and stood up and came back into the studio.

"Earlier," Susan said, "the light would have been on me. Did anyone drop anything? Like a cigarette of an unusual brand, imported specially for So and So?"

Keep it light, she thought. He looks worried. About me, I suppose.

"Nothing," Heimrich said, not rising to it. (He really must be worried, she thought.) "The ground's hard." He stood and looked at her, but she was not sure he saw her.

"It could," she said, "have been one of the reporters. Or photographers. Or—could it have been somebody posing as one of them?"

"Possibly," he said. "The latter. I can't see any reason why an actual reporter would want the design." He regarded the nude. "That, maybe," he said. "Not the design. Anyway, Crowley—" He let it trail off. "Somebody else. Somebody who watched you. You're sure you can't remember who was in the station wagon you had to back for?"

She was sure. She said she had already told him she was sure. If lightness wouldn't work, then—

"Now Susan," Heimrich said. "The point is, it couldn't have been whoever was in the station wagon. I mean, if somebody watched you. Couldn't investigate then because the reporters were here. Come back later, when they had left. Because whoever was in the wagon was a long time on his way and—"

"Wait," Susan said. "I forgot. There was another station wagon. Green, like the first one."

She told him of the tail of a station wagon which had rounded a curve ahead of her as she was driving toward home on Sugar Creek Lane. Which must have been—she paused for an estimate—at least twenty minutes after the first wagon had turned down the lane from the Collins driveway and, presumably, gone on its way. She said, "Presumably." She stumbled over it.

"Yes," Heimrich said. "Did you have Colonel with you?"

She merely raised eyebrows at that, widened eyes.

"Colonel stands out," Heimrich said. "On that front seat—"

"Oh," she said. "He was. And—he goes to the shop most days. Always now Michael's at camp. And sits a good deal of the time looking out the door, where anybody can see him. So even somebody who didn't know me, didn't recognize me could—put two and two together. Colonel and me."

"Yes," Heimrich said. "And, seeing you driving up toward the house—seeing Colonel anyway—and perhaps having heard some place that we—well—"

She waited a moment, to no purpose.

"Are casual acquaintances," she said. "That if I found something of revealing importance, I might just happen to mention it to you."

And she finally made him smile. Not for long, not freely, but smile.

"You put it very well," Heimrich told her. "And—parked the car, walked back up, not necessarily along the drive—there may be a path—watched you through the window—ducked when you started to leave. I suppose it took you a few minutes to get your car out from among the others?"

"Not long," she said. "Yes, I'd think he'd have had time to get back to his car. If there's a path, especially. Of course, I'm not sure it was the same car." She shook her head. "First," she said, "I leave the door unlocked. Would he have known that? Because, I take it, you think he went away without the design—didn't come in as soon as my back was turned and grab it?"

"He may have done that," Heimrich said. "He would have been cutting it pretty fine. Also, there were a good many people around by then. I'd guess, if it was the man in the station wagon—and it's all guessing, naturally—he thought it over after he left and decided to come back. He may have planned to force the door. Finding it unlocked was just a fortunate accident. Then—" He ended with a shrug. "All hypothesis," he said. "Blow on it—poof. Probably it'll turn out that Collins killed her and then himself."

"And the design?" Susan asked. "Stolen and destroyed by an outraged art lover."

"Now Susan."

"It couldn't be," she said, "that you are just trying to reassure a—"

And a siren sounded, gently, very briefly. It was as nearly apologetic as a siren can make itself. They went back through the house and found Trooper Crowley about to come into it. He stopped, more or less at attention, more or less worried. He said, "Something wrong, captain?"

"A little something," Heimrich said. "Not your fault, that I can see. But a couple of things you can clear up. First—somebody picked up the Buick wagon. Who?"

"But I thought you said—" Crowley began, and Heimrich interrupted, said, "I did, Crowley. Perfectly all right for somebody to get the car. Who was it?"

And there was the first catch. Crowley didn't know.

His assigned task was to see that the reporters got in, see that they didn't carry the house away when they left, lock up after them. He had got there half an hour or so before the reporters were due, on the chance that some one of them might be prompter than the rest, might seek to get ahead of the rest. He had got out and walked around, and sought a breeze. He looked at Heimrich.

"Sure," Heimrich said. "And?"

He had gone out on the terrace to which, with the sliding glass panels open, the swimming pool opened. He had stood there, where there was a breeze of sorts, and looked down at the Hudson. There had been a little sailboat on the Hudson. He had been where, if he heard a sound, he could look back and see the head of the driveway, and anybody coming up it in a car.

He had heard a sound—the sound of a motor starting. He had gone back around the house and had been just in time to see the station wagon starting down the drive. He had not been in time to see who drove it.

"I'm sorry, captain. I—"

There had been, Heimrich told him, no reason for him to think, then, that the driver of the car mattered. Marley could come for the car, send someone for it. He had been told that.

"Of course," Crowley said, "I wondered why he'd walked up from the road, as he must have. Because somebody must have driven him over from the Center. But it didn't seem important. I supposed whoever drove the man who got the wagon had let him out at the foot of the drive. And—"

He looked more worried than before.

"Probably did," Heimrich said. "Nothing out of the way about it. Then?"

Then Mrs. Faye had come. He had let her in. A few minutes later, the first of the reporters and photographers arrived. He arranged that they wouldn't block Mrs. Faye's car off from the driveway. He had gone in with them and stood, as a sentinel, in living room and studio, and gone out with a couple of them to look at the pool. When they showed signs of being ready to go, he had gone back out to the turnaround and more or less counted them out.

"Mrs. Faye's car had gone by then?"

It had.

"I didn't see you go out, Mrs. Faye," Crowley said. "Maybe I was out by the pool."

"None of the reporters carried anything out?" Heimrich said. "Rolled up paper, probably. About so long?" He measured in the air with his hands.

"No," Crowley said. "I'd have stopped— So that's what's wrong? The picture of Miss Belford in the—" He stopped.

"No," Heimrich said. "A roll of paper, not canvas. You're sure, Crowley?"

"Nobody carried anything out he didn't carry in," Crowley said. "I'll swear to that."

"All right," Heimrich said. "You locked up after them?"

He had. He had closed and secured the panels between pool and terrace, locked the back door—"the kitchen door"—locked the front door; gone back on patrol. As instructed.

"The door from the studio?" Heimrich asked him. "Not the one into the house. The outside door?"

He was looked at blankly for a moment.

"Captain," Crowley said then, "I'm sorry as hell. Nobody told me there was a door there but I—I should have checked."

"Yes," Heimrich said. "Also, somebody should have told you about it."

Crowley did not look much comforted.

"You mean one of them carried this roll of paper out that way?" he said. "And—no. I counted them in, counted them out. Nobody carried anything. And they all went." But then he lost confidence. "I suppose," he said, "somebody could have carried it out and put it in the car when I was inside and gone back into the house. Only—well, it never entered my mind that anybody would want to steal anything, captain. And reporters don't—"

"All right," Heimrich said. "I don't blame you particularly. Although—"

"I'm sorry as hell, captain," Crowley said.

"Now Ray," Heimrich said. "Forget it. Anyway, I don't think, either, that it was one of the reporters. Somebody who came back after you had gone. Been seen going. You didn't pass a car on your way out? A car coming this way?"

Crowley hadn't. Which meant nothing; there were three roads, none of them direct, none to be chosen above another, from the Center to the house on the hilltop.

"When you were walking around," Heimrich said, "waiting for the press to show up, you didn't happen to come across a path? A path leading down to the road?"

Crowley brightened at that. He had; he showed Heimrich, while Susan waited on the front terrace. Heimrich came back and nodded.

"Steep," he said. "Goes straight down. Much quicker for a man on foot than the driveway. About half as long. And comes up on the far side of the house, where Crowley here wouldn't have seen anyone from the pool terrace. How whoever came for the Buick came, probably. Perhaps the second time, too."

Heimrich told Crowley he could get back on patrol. He told him not to worry. And to lock up, first. All doors, this time.

It shouldn't, Heimrich said, as they rolled slowly down the driveway, leaving Crowley to his locking up, be difficult to find out who had picked up the wagon since two people had to have been involved, and unless one was willing to lie for the other. Nobody in his right mind would walk from the Center to Collins's house on a day as hot as this. And nobody can come in one car, and drive two away. And there was not, so far as Heimrich could see, any reason for whoever it was to have come surreptitiously on the first visit. The second—

"Only," Susan said, "it doesn't have to be the same man, really. The first one—the one who saw me—might have mentioned what he'd seen to somebody else. A sort of 'Saw a funny thing up at the Collins house. Wonder what she was up to' sort of thing."

Heimrich looked doubtful; he said that it was, of course, possible. He turned the car east in Sugar Creek Lane.

"Of course," Susan Faye said. "Young Mr. Latham is an actor. And the girl even more so, isn't she? So I suppose they might think of that—re-enactment. Or she might and he humor her. He's very fond of her, of course. Might, I think, do almost anything she asked him to."

IX

Susan had promised to take care of herself; had pointed out that there was always Colonel. Heimrich, looking at the large, sad dog, had said, to that, "Well—" in a voice of doubt. Colonel, while perhaps courageous in his fashion, was a dog obviously resigned to disaster; a fatalistic dog, unlikely to intervene in a cause he would assume already lost. "Anyway," Susan said, "with the design gone, and probably ashes by now, it's only my word. Not even that—only my critical judgment. Why would that worry anybody?"

It wouldn't, Heimrich told himself, driving toward the Center. The design itself had been the danger, not what anyone could describe of it. The design had been taken care of, no longer existed, even as a hint. Susan was not a danger to anyone, and so not in danger from anyone. Also she was an intelligent woman, not likely to take needless risk. Intelligent and observant, and to be trusted. She had, more quickly than he, realized how young George Latham felt about even younger Chris Waggoner. An attractive couple they made, as people said. Heimrich had, of course, to consider also whether they might not be a conspiratorial couple.

It was obvious that the re-enactment—on the face of it slightly absurd—need not be the only purpose of their visit to the Collins house. It might have been a spur-of-the-moment tableau, arranged for the delection of whoever was audibly approaching in a laboring car on a steep driveway.

It was not necessary to believe that Chris and Latham had gone to the house so that she could lie on a tile floor in a bathing suit, and in the posture of a murdered girl. They could have gone to get the fabric design because it threatened one of them, or both of them.

They could have got it, put it in the Chevrolet convertible, driven unmolested away with it before its absence was discovered. And laughed lightheartedly up their sleeves. (Except, of course, that the girl wasn't wearing sleeves.)

Actors, Heimrich thought morosely, turning down Van Brunt Avenue toward the Center, toward the Inn. It was to be anticipated that in any murder investigation one would encounter at least one liar, and might expect to come across several. But, in the usual course, they would be only layman liars. Here he was confronted with a handful of people who, it might be said, lied for a living. Perhaps the word was harsh; the fact was inescapable. An actor lives by pretending—with voice, with facial muscles, with the whole of the body—to be someone he is not. A director, a producer, lives by creating a semblance which is not a fact. Heimrich felt rather put upon; he was conscious of kinship with Colonel.

For all he knew, Latham had been acting—and had fooled them both—when he put an arm around Chris Waggoner, and she acting when she, momentarily, seemed to soften in his arm. And Dale acting when he denied any residual passion for Peggy Belford. And Chris again when her eyes widened in apparent uneasiness at something she had thought about Peggy's possible knowledge of the whereabouts of bodies. And Marley. And Zersk. And, for all he knew, Burt Alder of publicity, who might have acquired acting ability by osmosis.

It would, Heimrich thought—driving slowly down Van Brunt Avenue, through Sunday afternoon traffic—be much simpler to accept the semblance as the fact, and nobody would blame him if he did. The county district attorney would, certainly, be among those who would not blame him, since district attorneys much prefer not to be asked to make bricks without straw, and since Heimrich certainly had not, at the moment, straw to offer. Oh—one wisp. A fabric design which he could not produce, and a young woman's opinion that a color in it was "wrong." Considering this, Heimrich felt more than ever as he supposed Colonel habitually to feel, and thought that he probably now looked like Colonel. (Instead of like a hippopotamus.)

And yet that straw was the major thing which Heimrich, being who he was, still had to clutch at; the only tangible (but no longer that) evidence that he was confronted not with the fact of murder and suicide but with contrivance. Well—since he had nothing more, he might as well see whether he could come up with an hypothesis which would explain the wrongness of the red in the design. Start with the simplest thing—red is for danger. Then Collins—assuming it was he who had daubed the red on the design—wanted to convey the fact of danger. Presumably, to himself. Possibly, to Peggy Belford.

Heimrich shook this in his mind. It seemed a solid grain, if a small one. Then, why? Putting red paint on paper could not ward off danger. At any rate, Heimrich could not see how it could. And, most obviously, it had not. So—

Red is a warning; it is also an admonition to stop. Then—to stop before accepting what appeared, before confusing semblance with fact? An obscure way of doing it, certainly; a subtlety likely to be overlooked altogether. Except—Collins had known Susan was coming; that a policeman probably would be with her. So he could count on Susan's seeing that the color was wrong, passing the fact on to the policeman. If there were something for the policeman to concern himself with.

Why the indirection? Because, presumably, the direct was impossible, would not be allowed. Now, Heimrich thought, I may be getting somewhere. He turned into the almost-filled parking lot of the Old Stone Inn, but did not at once leave the car. He shut the motor off and continued with hypothesis. What he needed, clearly, was a series of events which included an opportunity to daub glaring red on paper but not to leave an explicit message; a series of events which did not, obviously include the murder of Peggy Belford by Collins and the murder of Collins by himself. Which, therefore, included at least one other person. A person who knew that Peggy was at the Collins house and that, for at least an hour, Collins himself was not. Which included, apparently, practically everyone. Except Roland Fielding?

So— Peggy had gone to the house for a swim. Start with that, which was obvious. Collins had had a swim with her, which was probable, although not certain. Collins had left at about three-thirty to drive into the Center. He had returned about four-thirty and— found Peggy dead? And somebody standing over her with a gun? And had said, "I realize you've got to kill me too, but do you mind if I put a finishing touch on a design I'm doing before you do?" That was fairly absurd. Found Peggy still alive, but someone with a gun with her and—and what? Heimrich could not think; he closed his eyes and, after a time, shook his head.

Not found her there at all because—because she was dead, and her body hidden? Heimrich's interest quickened somewhat. Found her murderer there and been told, by him, that Peggy had gone off somewhere and that he was waiting for her—and been lulled by this? And the murderer's purpose? Instead of merely killing and going, leaving a cadaver for Collins to explain.

Because, before he could do that, he had heard Collins's car coming up the drive? Jeeps make a good deal of noise. Had had time only to hide the body? In a closet? Possibly only in the kitchen. Assuming that, his reason for not shooting Collins immediately? His reason for lulling him, getting him to wait, also, for the presumptive return of a girl who was already dead?

Uh-huh, Heimrich said to himself. Collins could not be shot down out of hand. He had to be maneuvered into a position which would support the theory—create the semblance—of suicide. Until that had been done, Collins must not suspect.

But—suppose Collins had? Perhaps only vaguely suspected, uneasily suspected. A bulge in the man's pocket? Or, conceivably, the odor of powder still in the air? (The conditioning unit would, however, have taken it out quickly.) Skip that; outline now, fill in later, if possible. Suppose, further, that Collins had concealed his suspicion, his uneasiness. Said that, while they waited, he might as well finish off a thing he was doing in the studio. Hoping, probably, to get into the studio alone; perhaps even get his gun out of the table drawer.

The murderer would not have let him go alone. That was obvious. So anything Collins might do to show danger, to say to someone, all else failing, that the way it looked was not the way it was, would have had to be done under watchful, hostile eyes. No chance, obviously, to write it plain—to write out, somewhere, "So and So has, I think, killed Peggy Belford. He is, unless I can prevent it, going to kill me. He will probably try to make it appear that I killed her and then myself."

The Manual of Procedure of the Police Department of the City of New York says that a good detective must have "the ability to draw upon the imagination." Heimrich drew on his, played the scene in his mind.

A man—say it was a man; keep it simple—sitting and watching, his manner easy, his hand on a gun in his pocket. "Want to touch up this color," Collins said, in the scene Heimrich's imagination wrote for him. "A bit drab, don't you think? Needs some life in it," the while mixing colors until red glared in them, transferring red to drawing paper. "Looks better now, don't you think?" Collins said, in Heimrich's mind. "Much better," the murderer said, in Heimrich's mind—and in whose voice? Marley's deep voice; Dale's modulated voice; Zersk's jagged voice? In George Latham's agreeable baritone? Or—in one of the voices of Chris Waggoner? (There was nothing in this imagined sequence impossible to an active girl.)

Heimrich's imagination could not cast the part. Write the scene first, people it later.

"Much better," the voice without identity said. "Oh—I think I hear her in the living room. Better go back and see, hadn't we?"

Shift the scene, now. Shift it to the living room. The dialogue? "I could have sworn I heard her," in the voice without identity. "Well, may as well sit down while we wait, hadn't we? Hate to impose but I've got to get in touch with her as soon as possible." Because there's a message for her at the Inn? Because there's a last-minute change in a scene and we have to go over it for tomorrow? Because the last shot didn't come out the way we wanted and we've got to do it over right away? Because—there was no use worrying about that.

And Collins, still wary, still pretending to suspect nothing—still playing for time, having only time to play for. *No.* Wait. Having a definite thing to play for—the arrival of Mrs. Susan Faye, accompanied by Captain M. L. Heimrich, New York State Police. If we had left half an hour earlier, Heimrich thought; perhaps only fifteen minutes earlier. Which was wasting thought.

Collins, wary, playing for time—but not wary enough, running out of time. In the last seconds, somehow tricked—caught in a moment of unwariness. Come at quickly before he could get out of a chair; a gun hard and for an instant cold against his temple and then—nothing. Or a horrible, unimaginable, roaring of pain? No use guessing about that. In one way or another, all sometime learn, and in no way can any report.

The last bit of action, Heimrich thought, was a little tricky, a little hard to visualize. How get that close to a suspicious man? Possibly, of course, by holding a gun on him. Merely that. Any man, his life threatened, will play for a second more of life, an

instant more. Play to the end in the disbelief of the living that
death has come; in the hope, however dim, that some instant's action
may hold death off.

Heimrich shook the hypothesis in his mind. It more or less held
together. As, he thought with some gloom, why shouldn't it? Since
I made it up, as a playwright might. Apparently he, also, was susceptible to osmosis. A tendency to be watched, he thought.

To prove the hypothesis, to say nothing of casting what was, for
him, the central role, he had to have more. (Or, of course, think
better.) But he could not see that, as things stood, there was more
to be found. It was, he decided, desirable that more be added. The
theft of the design was, he trusted, a start in that direction. And the
presence at the house of Chris Waggoner and her handsome young
man—if her young man—was perhaps a start. It was, however, possible that this had been only a way chosen by youth to while away
a peaceful Sunday afternoon. There is not a great deal to do in Van
Brunt Center on a Sunday afternoon, for those in transit through it.
(Residents play games; drink drinks; sometimes work in gardens.)

It was, Heimrich decided, time to stir up the animals. He wished
he knew which animals to stir.

He got out of the car. He might as well see if the Buick station
wagon had got safely home, assuming the Inn's parking lot was
home. And assuming he would know it if he saw it. Lucky it wasn't a
Ford, or a Chevy, he thought, beginning a leisurely tour of the parking lot. They were everywhere. Along with Volkswagens. And here
a Jag and there a Jag and—

And here a green Buick station wagon, with city license plates.
Not, evidently, driven east from California. Bought here for Marley's eastern occasions, which might indicate that Marley had more
money than Anton Zersk had thought. Or that he was on an expense
account of some proportions. Or that the car really belonged to

Allied Pictures. Or, of course, that it was another station wagon entirely.

Heimrich looked into the back of the station wagon and instantly felt slightly ridiculous. There was a motor scooter, very small and bright and neat, in the back of the wagon. So whoever had gone to get the wagon had not had to be driven by anybody. His identity was, therefore, his to reveal or hide. Unless they could turn up somebody who had seen somebody aboard a scooter bouncing along a country road. He might as well start with Paul Marley, he thought, and went in through the taproom, where reporters drank contentedly. They rose as one.

"Nothing," Heimrich told them and then hesitated. "That is— nothing I can give you now." Which made them flutter. Heimrich was firm. "Not now," he said. "Sorry."

"Apparently," the *Daily Mirror* told him, "it's not as open and shut as you thought. Or, wanted us to think you thought."

"Well," Heimrich said. "I don't know that I want to go that far."

"Hint of new developments," the *Daily Mirror* said. "Reason to believe the police are not entirely satisfied."

Heimrich could not remember having previously met a reporter who talked as it was to be presumed he wrote. It took, Heimrich thought, all kinds.

"I can't stop you," Heimrich said. "There may be something later."

"Make it tomorrow," the *Journal American* told him. "Give the afternoons a break, for a change."

"How about coming up to the house and pointing at something? For the mobile unit?"

That was NBC. Or perhaps CBS.

"Perhaps tomorrow," Heimrich said, and left, and the press sought telephones. Which was what Heimrich had had in mind. Burt Alder followed him. He said, with asperity, that he supposed Heimrich knew what he'd done.

"Now Mr. Alder," Heimrich said. "M. G. will be fit to be tied, naturally."

Paul Marley was in The Suite, which he shared with Francis Dale. Dale was not. Marley was at a table in the living room, working on what Heimrich took to be a script. He took off heavy-rimmed eyeglasses and pushed back his blond hair and looked at Heimrich.

"I see," Heimrich said, "that you picked up the station wagon."

"Sure," Marley said, in his amazingly deep voice. "You said it would be—"

"I know," Heimrich said. "Get it yourself, Mr. Marley?"

"Sure," Marley said. "Why not? Does it make a difference?"

Since it was so readily admitted, it probably didn't make any difference, Heimrich thought. Which was somewhat disappointing, although he had been prepared for it.

"Just keeping things straight," he told the big man, mildly. "Went up there on the scooter?"

Marley had. And, again, what difference did it make?

Heimrich did not answer that. He said, "And left the scooter down on the road and walked up to the house?"

Marley couldn't see what Heimrich was getting at, what he was making a point of. The driveway was steep and rough, more than the scooter could handle. "With a man my size on it."

"Walked up the drive? Or the path?"

"Now listen," Marley said. "What's this all about? And what path? You said it was O.K. to get the wagon and—"

"Just getting things straight," Heimrich said. "Coming down the drive in the Buick you met a young woman coming up?"

"Yes. A woman with a damn big dog on the seat. She had to back down."

"Then?"

"This is damned pointless," Marley said. "But all right. Went down the road a few yards to where I'd put the scooter off to the side. So somebody wouldn't run over it. Loaded it into the wagon and came back here. Had lunch here. For lunch I had shirred eggs and sausage and—"

"Now Mr. Marley," Heimrich said. "I realize this seems trivial. How long did it take you to load the scooter?"

"Maybe you know what you're after," Marley said, in a tone of doubt, but of resignation. "Five minutes or so. Maybe ten. It's heavier than it looks and you've got to get it set so it won't roll around."

"You didn't go back to the house later?" Heimrich said. "To, say, pick up something you'd forgotten?"

"I certainly did not. And now suppose you tell me what the hell you are after."

Heimrich hesitated. He let an expression of doubt, of indecision, appear on his face. He thought how much more adeptly almost any of these people, including Marley, could arrange on a face an expression suitable to the occasion.

"Well—" Heimrich said. "I suppose there's no harm in saying this much. Somebody's been poking around up there. Seems the door got left unlocked somehow."

"Poking around? Took something, you mean?"

"That's just it," Heimrich said. "Something no good to anyone. Design for a fabric. Collins had done it to show to Mrs. Faye. Susan Faye. She was the young woman with the dog. On her way up to have a second look at the design. Been a bit shaken up after we found the bodies, naturally. Didn't really look at it."

He sounded puzzled. He said it didn't seem to make much sense, but that there it was. Why anybody would want to steal a fabric design—

It was time for a slip.

"Whatever Mrs. Faye felt was wrong," Heimrich said, in an abstracted tone, "it certainly didn't have anything to do with—"

He caught himself. He looked (he hoped) somewhat embarrassed.

"Wrong?" Marley said.

"All right," Heimrich said, "I said more than I meant to. Mrs. Faye got one of those notions women get. Thought there was something wrong in the studio. Something there that oughtn't to be, or the other way around. It's all very vague. Something that didn't belong in—"

Again he stopped and shook his head in self-reproof.

"Wait a minute," Marley said, which was what Heimrich was already doing. "Something to do with the—deaths? Something that didn't belong in the picture, you were going to say?"

"Now Mr. Marley—"

"Wrong with the setup," Marley said. "Makes you not so sure Collins killed Peggy, the way it looked?"

"Well—"

Marley would be damned. He got up from the table.

"This vague—feeling—of this Mrs. Faye," he said. "That's all you've got to go on?"

"Well," Heimrich said. "The chief thing, I suppose."

"And she doesn't know what it was? Only 'something' in the studio?" He shook his big head. "That sounds a lot like intuition to me," he said.

"Yes," Heimrich said. "Of course, it's more or less Mrs. Faye's line of country. Spot things you and I wouldn't, perhaps."

"But," Marley said, "in spite of being so vague about it, she's sure it wasn't this—what did you call it—design?"

"Seems to be."

Marley didn't get it. Why, he wanted to know, would anybody—he supposed Heimrich meant somebody with something to hide about the murder—steal a design that hadn't anything to do with anything? Why, come to that, think it had something to do with something?

"I wish I knew," Heimrich said. "We'll just have to keep plugging, apparently. I'm afraid Mrs. Faye's memory won't improve. She doesn't think it will. Anyway, you say it wasn't you."

Marley said it sure as hell wasn't.

Heimrich was sorry he'd interrupted Mr. Marley's work. He would just have to keep asking around. Did Mr. Marley know where he could find the others? Mr. Dale? Miss Waggoner? Mr. Latham? Mr. Zersk, although of course Mr. Zersk wasn't staying at the hotel.

Dale had driven into New York to have lunch with somebody. Marley didn't, he said, know about the others. He hoped to God young Georgie-Porgie was working on a scene he couldn't seem to get through his head. He hoped with Zersk.

Stir up the animals. It was hard to be sure whether he had stirred up Mr. Marley. It had not been apparent. He had, he suspected, merely persuaded Mr. Marley that the case was in the hands of extremely doddering detectives.

He found Anton Zersk and George Latham together, as Marley had hoped. They were not, however, working on a scene, unless the scene included badminton, which Heimrich doubted had been played in the old Dutch days along the Hudson. Bowling would have been more like it. Zersk and young Latham were being noticeably athletic on the badminton court of the Cold Harbor Motor Lodge.

Heimrich doddered for their benefit. Neither had stolen the roll of drawing paper. Both were suitably puzzled as to what purpose such a theft would have served; properly, but no more than properly (so far as Heimrich could determine), interested in, and blank about, what Susan Faye could have seen wrong in the studio.

"Chris and I did go in there," Latham said. "Before we did that —re-enactment."

"By the way," Heimrich said, "Miss Waggoner's idea or yours? The re-enactment."

It had been hers; Latham smiled at it, in retrospect. He said that Chris had a lot of ideas.

They had gone into the studio to look at the nude portrait of Peggy Belford, having read about it in the newspapers. And?

"The guy sure could paint," Latham said.

They had, certainly, taken nothing out of the studio.

Where, now, was Miss Waggoner? If she wasn't at the hotel, where Latham had taken her after they left the Collins house, neither knew.

"She might have noticed something in the studio," Heimrich said. "Maybe it was something only a woman would notice. Mind asking her, if you see her before I do?"

This was, primarily, to Latham, who certainly would ask her. Although, if it had been anything obvious, he supposed she would have mentioned it at the time.

Heimrich drove back to the Inn. Miss Waggoner was not in her room, nor in any of the public rooms. Forniss, however, was in the taproom, meditatively consuming beer.

X

THE REPORTERS HAD left the taproom, apparently in a pack. Reporters have a tendency to move in packs. Heimrich moved into the taproom's coolness and joined Forniss, at the table, in a beer.

"Our friend Fielding was here yesterday," Forniss said. "Looking for Miss Belford." Forniss's voice reflected some satisfaction. Heimrich said, "Oh?" encouragingly.

Forniss had come back to the Inn half an hour ago, after most of an afternoon at a telephone. To which he would come later. He had been hailed from the desk by Miss Sneed—Miss Amantha Sneed, the Inn's bookkeeper, filling in at the desk for a couple of quiet afternoon hours, as she did a good many afternoons. As she had done the afternoon before. Miss Sneed had said, "Oh! Sergeant Forniss." Forniss had gone over.

"Oh," Miss Sneed said, "I don't suppose it's anything. But there was a man here yesterday when I was on enquiring about Miss Belford. Oh, the poor thing."

The "poor thing," it appeared, had been Miss Belford, not the enquiring man.

The man had asked whether Miss Belford was registered there and, on being told she was, had asked her room number and, being given it, had used the house phone. And had been unanswered. He had looked into the public rooms—into the taproom, the lounge— and, shaking his head, gone out.

"Fielding?" Heimrich said, and Forniss said, "Listen."

"Who does this sound like?" Forniss said. " 'Portly man.' 'Very' portly. Partly bald. Wasn't wearing a hat. Noticeably husky voice. Wore glasses. Rimless bifocals. Miss Sneed had seen him before.

Thought he was a local who has dinner here now and then. Not one of the regulars; doesn't think he actually lives in Van Brunt. Sort of a semi-local, apparently."

"Observant woman Miss Sneed," Heimrich said. "Still— Although I'll admit it fits."

"So," Forniss said, "I found Mrs. Oliphant. Told her what Miss Sneed said. Mrs. Oliphant said, 'Goodness. That must have been Mr. Fielding,' and told me that Mr. Fielding and Miss Belford had been married, she understood, and divorced. And said, 'Goodness, these movie people,' and then that she shouldn't have said that, with poor Miss Belford dead and all like that."

Mrs. Oliphant is the owner of the Old Stone Inn. She finds "all like that" a convenient catch-all, although it is sometimes difficult to determine what she has caught in it.

Heimrich said, "Hm-mm." He pointed out that none of this placed Roland Fielding at the Collins house, with a gun in his hand.

"Nope," Forniss said. "But—somebody could have told him where she was. Also, he'd know about Collins. And the house. And, probably, the swimming pool. And that Belford liked swimming pools." He paused. "Two thousand a month is still a lot of money," Forniss said.

"We'll ask him," Heimrich said. "Also, what he was doing this afternoon. Since—"

Forniss listened.

"Huh-uh," Forniss said. "Mrs. Faye went there about ten? The first time. And—about ten we were talking to Fielding. So, he couldn't have looked in the window and watched her. Only—you're sure somebody did?"

"Now Charlie. No."

"Could be," Forniss said, "our going there worried him. Got him to wondering. Had he missed something when he killed them? Left something that might give him away? And, remembered that Collins had worked on the design while he was there—while they were supposed to be waiting for La Belford."

"Which," Heimrich said, "is pure, unadulterated theory, Charlie."

"Yep," Forniss said. "Wondered if maybe there had been something phony about that, like maybe Collins had left a message and he'd missed it. So he goes up to see, on the chance he can get in and look, and if there's somebody around, he's a sightseer. What the newspaper boys call morbidly curious. They having done their damnedest to stir up the curiosity."

"Hm-mm," Heimrich said.

"That way," Forniss said, "we get around his not watching Mrs. Faye through the window."

"We'll ask him," Heimrich said. "Also—see that he knows the design was the wrong thing to steal."

Forniss lighted a cigarette. He raised heavy eyebrows.

Heimrich told him of the stirring up of animals.

"Only," Forniss said, "suppose our man, instead of going back to the house to have another look, goes to Mrs. Faye and—tries to persuade her to remember?"

"Let's hope not," Heimrich said. "I made it pretty definite that she'd tried to remember and couldn't. That she didn't think she was going to be able to. The sensible thing would be to go to the house and look."

"Let's hope our man is sensible," Forniss said. "Now, about L.A."

About L.A., as reported upon, via telephone, by Ben Cohen, et al., at considerable toll cost to the New York State Police:

If Heimrich thought, or had hoped, that there was something suspicious about the death from too much Nembutal of Gertrude Marley, Forniss was afraid Heimrich was going to be disappointed. The police were satisfied; beyond that, the press was satisfied. Forniss was satisfied himself.

Mrs. Marley had taken the Nembutal on going to bed one night some eighteen months previously. Marley had been at home; he had been in his study going over a preliminary treatment of *The Last Patroon*. He had gone up to his own, adjoining room, around two o'clock in the morning, and had gone quietly so as not to waken his wife. It was not until ten o'clock the next morning that he discovered wakening her would have been impossible.

She had been depressed. Marley said that, and that he had not thought it serious. And a doctor said that, and that he had not thought it serious either, but that it was not always possible to tell. The doctor blamed himself.

Chris, not sixteen then, away at school, had not agreed—had insisted, with a child's desperate violence, desperate belief, that her mother would never have taken her own life, that death must have been accidental. The police had been tolerant; everybody had been tolerant. It had, formally, been left accident or suicide, since it did not much matter—since there was no suggestion of homicide.

"Too bad, in a way," Forniss said. "Marley kills his wife, La Belford finds out about it and puts the squeeze on and—exit La Belford. Nice simple pattern. Only, nothing to hang it on. Suicide while in a depression; state of depression verified by medical evidence."

"It would have been a nice pattern," Heimrich said. "The doctor *was* a doctor?"

Forniss raised his eyebrows.

"Psychiatrist?" Heimrich said. "They have some queer ones out there, from all I hear. An M.D.?"

"Oh," Forniss said. "Not an M.D., Cohen says. Psychoanalyst. Why?"

Forniss could consider it merely curiosity. That, plus the fact that they did have some queer ones out there. More than most places, possibly, although the "lay psychoanalyst" was not unknown elsewhere; was not, either, to be confused with a psychiatrist who might place great reliance on psychoanalytical theories and methods or might not. It probably didn't make any difference.

"This man," Forniss said. "A—" He referred to notes—"A Dr. Robert Wiley, is very popular with the movie people, Cohen says. You've had the Wiley treatment or you might as well be normal, and if you're normal, where are you?"

"Any of our little group?"

It was characteristic of Forniss that he had found out, although, in his own mind, accepting Mrs. Marley's death as suicidal; regarding things related to it as, therefore, of little importance. Zersk had been a patient of Dr. Wiley, Cohen had heard. He had never heard that Dale had been.

"By the way," Forniss said, interrupting himself, "Dale's real name, believe it or not, is Herman Dobbling. Or was, anyway." He paused. "Except that everybody knows that—I mean, if Belford had been, say, the only one—" He shrugged his shoulders.

He regarded his empty glass. He signaled to Harold, the barman.

"You know," Forniss said, "it could be that Collins was the one somebody was really after. You've thought of that?"

"Yes," Heimrich said. "The other seems more likely but, yes. So Zersk was a patient of this—doctor?"

"Yes. And Peggy went around with him, only not as a patient as far as Ben knows, for a while. After she was separated from Fielding. Instead, as everyone expected, with Marley."

"Expected?"

Cohen had said that there had been rumors. He said that there were always rumors about Peggy Belford. He also said that there had not been anything to prove that Peggy had not been a friend both of Marley and his wife, and there was nothing to make this association strange, since Peggy was frequently in pictures Marley produced. Had Cohen, incidentally, thought it strange that Peggy was so often in Marley pictures?

"Because she couldn't act?" Cohen had said. "Most of them can't. Most of them don't look like she looked."

Mrs. Marley's money had gone to her daughter, not to her husband. And her lawyer had been appointed Chris's guardian. And Marley, interviewed at the time of his wife's death, had said that this had long been arranged between them and that he had thought it eminently fair, since a large part of the money had been earned by Chris's father.

"For my money," Forniss said, "Mrs. Marley's death, and what she did with her money, doesn't hook up."

"Apparently not," Heimrich said. "Go ahead, Charlie."

Dale—whether once a Dobbling or not—was generally considered a good egg; indeed, a very superior egg. He had a big fruit ranch and, when not "working"—"they're only working when they're doing a picture," Forniss said—managed it himself. He had not remarried since Peggy had divorced him. "Apparently plays the field in a casual sort of way," Forniss said. Dale had paid Peggy alimony, reputedly large, until her marriage to Fielding, but the payments stopped with the marriage.

"Come back to Fielding all the time," Forniss pointed out and got a mild "Now Charlie," for his pains.

Zersk was more interesting. He had escaped, with his wife, from Czechoslovakia some ten years before. He had already, on the Continent, made a considerable reputation as a director, chiefly for the stage but also for motion pictures. "Got going early, apparently," Forniss said. "In his thirties now."

Zersk had taken out first papers. It would soon be time for him to become a citizen. He had directed, for Marley—and so for Allied Pictures—several films in which Peggy Belford appeared. It was rumored that he did not share Cohen's tolerant view of her acting. There were also rumors that M. G. Drisken did not.

"But," Cohen had said, "Marley's hot just now, so they let him have it his way pretty much. Anyway, as long as she's box office."

Forniss had said that Zersk was more interesting. Why?

Forniss hesitated. He said that he didn't, God knew, want to sound like the late senator. On the other hand—

There had, Cohen had told him, been rumors about Anton Zersk. Where they had started wasn't certain; those who scoffed at them said that they had begun in the active, and self-serving, imagination of another director.

"A very reformed character," Forniss said. "Name of Hooker— Bertram Hooker. When they were making a lot of fuss on the West Coast a few years back—when they were making a lot of fuss everywhere, come to that—this Hooker bared his chest. Bared a lot of other chests. Very co-operative witness. Every time they ran out of headlines there was good old Hooker, with more chests to bare."

"Zersk's?"

Not publicly. But, when the headlines began to taper off a bit and the committee—"state committee, this one was"—decided they had milked the thing dry, Hooker did a lot of private hinting. He could not, then, name names, since his charges were no longer privileged and a few people were showing signs of biting back, but he could start rumors. A good many started about that time and one of them concerned Zersk. Whether Hooker actually started it—

"Specifically?"

"That Zersk and his wife weren't really refugees from the Iron Curtain. That their escape, which seems to have got a good deal of publicity, only I don't remember it, was rigged. That actually, they were agents, sent over to pervert the pure stream of American movies. You know the sort of stuff. Only—"

He paused, considered.

"Countries use agents," he said. "Always have and always will, I guess. That the two hundred percenters see a dozen under every bush doesn't mean that there isn't one under every hundredth bush, does it? That Hooker obviously did a lot of lying—even the committee began to suspect that, finally—doesn't mean he was always lying. Sometimes, maybe, he had the goods. And—"

Again he paused.

"Miss Belford got around a lot," he said. "She was a real get-around girl. One of the people she got around with was this Hooker, Ben says. Nothing exclusive about it. Miss Belford wasn't what you'd call an exclusive girl. But if Hooker *did* happen to have something and *did* happen to pass it along to Belford. Well—"

"If she knew where anybody's buried a body," Heimrich said. "I quote the kids—young Latham, Chris the tragedy queen. And—more pure and unadulterated theory, Charlie."

"Yep," Forniss said, and reverted. "Two grand a month is a nice solid chunk of motive," he said. "Fielding's the one we know she really had where it hurts. You don't buy him?"

At the moment, Heimrich neither bought nor rejected. He collected samples. Did Forniss have more to offer?

Forniss thought he hadn't.

"The kid. Chris?"

Forniss looked at him a little blankly.

"I gather from what your friend Cohen says," Heimrich told his sergeant, "somewhat from what Dale says, that Chris was very devoted to her mother. If she got the idea that Miss Belford had—well, say moved in. That it was because of her moving in that Mrs. Marley killed herself. Chris dramatizes things, you know."

"You think of the damnedest things," Forniss said. "That was eighteen months ago."

"Children brood," Heimrich said. "Also—it was during the last few weeks, I gather, that Dale had been showing interest in Miss Belford. And Chris has a crush on Dale. The child could have thought Peggy was moving in again and that once was enough and—" He shrugged. He finished his beer.

"There was, if you're right, a good deal of dragging around of the body," Forniss said. "Awkward things, bodies."

"Yes," Heimrich said. "Of course, she was a little woman. And the place has got tiled floors—waxed tile. A bit slippery. And girls like Chris often have pretty good muscles underneath." He closed his eyes briefly. "I've heard," he said, opening them again. He regarded the opposite wall of the taproom.

Sergeant Forniss watched him, noted that he seemed to find much of interest in a reasonably uninteresting wall. It was a little, Forniss thought, as if Heimrich saw daylight there. Forniss also looked at the wall. One of the pictures needed straightening. It could hardly be that.

"I tell you what we'll do, Charlie," Heimrich said. "You go ask Mr. Fielding if he found Miss Belford yesterday afternoon. I'll go ask Mr. Zersk if he's a Russian agent. And Mr. Dale, if I run into him, if he's entirely sure that he didn't expect Miss Belford to bounce in his direction when she bounced off Fielding. Annoying to be disappointed, it might have been."

Forniss looked at him, raised eyebrows.

"Also," Heimrich said, "you might tell Fielding the one about the mistake somebody made in stealing the design. And I'll make sure the word has got to Mr. Dale. By the way, make it clear—very clear —that Mrs. Faye is sure she'll never remember what she thought was wrong. And have young Crowley get out of uniform for a little chore. And—" He looked at his watch. "We'll meet here around six-thirty," he said. "I imagine we'll get a telephone call."

XI

ANTON ZERSK SAID he was not a Russian agent, or a Czech agent or any kind of agent and that Bertram Hooker was a rat—several kinds of a rat, which he duly listed. Zersk bristled; his harsh hair seemed to stand more than ever on end. He said he was damned tired of the whole business, and especially of people like Bertram Hooker. He said that if Hooker had done his song and dance—type qualified; fully explained—for Peggy Belford he, Zersk, knew nothing about it, because Peggy had never brought it up.

He walked up and down his room at the Cold Harbor Motor Lodge and glared at Heimrich, who sat and listened—who, when Zersk bristled with especial fervor, said, "Now Mr. Zersk" in a soothing tone. Zersk was not a man who soothed readily.

"Also," Zersk said—and in the tricky word Heimrich for the first time detected a hint of alien accent—"Also, suppose she had and had tried to make something of it? I don't say she wouldn't, but what did she have? Something somebody else had told her. If I wanted to kill anybody, it would be Hooker himself, wouldn't it?" He glared. "Wouldn't I?" he repeated. He lighted a cigarette. "Which," he said, "I may do when I get back to the Coast. On general principles. High time somebody did."

"Now Mr. Zersk."

"Also," Zersk said, "don't think the FBI didn't check me out when this stuff started to go around. And, told me to forget it. Ask them."

"All right," Heimrich said. "A lot of things crop up in this sort of business. We have to go round clearing them up. Wastes a lot of time, but there it is."

Heimrich left—left Zersk still glaring. It seemed likely, it seemed very probable, that he had wasted time. Which was part of the trade. All the same—

Heimrich stopped in a telephone booth. He told Hawthorne to send through a request to Washington for any information available on one Zersk, Anton, who had escaped from Czechoslovakia with his wife by—as Heimrich now vaguely recalled—taking over part of a train. That did not seem improbable; Zersk, Heimrich thought, could dispense with a locomotive, himself provide driving power. He had it to spare.

Heimrich got to the Inn's taproom at six-thirty and found that, as he had hoped, the audience was adequate. The newspaper people were back, including reporters for the networks. That was excellent; news travels fastest that travels by air. Francis Dale and Paul Marley were having drinks together; George Latham and Chris had a table and Chris had a glass filled darkly. Heimrich trusted with Coke. He would hate to see Harold, the barman, get into trouble. Harold was not a man likely to.

The press swarmed around Heimrich, who shook his head sadly and seemed a man preoccupied. He was told that he had as good as promised a story; that he had hinted at new developments. He was a man discouraged, apologetic. If he had, things had changed. He was a man for whom things had worked out badly; a man whose antici-pated fish had got away. "Police appear baffled," the *Daily Mirror* said, resentfully, and went to the bar. "Promised disclosures fail to materialize. Bourbon and water."

Heimrich nodded to Dale, to Marley, a man deep in worried thought. He said, "Hello" to Latham, to Chris, and shook his head sadly. He found a table and awaited Forniss, who arrived in ten minutes, and arrived with shaking head. They ordered, glumly.

Forniss talked briefly, in a lowered voice, the voice of a man who has met adversity. His words were audible only to Heimrich. Field-ing had admitted, grumpily, that he had asked for Peggy Belford at the Inn the previous afternoon; denied, with more vigor, that he had found her; admitted he knew Collins slightly—"both members of the Peggy club," Fielding said; denied that he had thought Peggy might have gone to Collins's house, and that he had gone there to look for her. He also said that he was getting damn tired of being badgered, and if they wanted to make something of it to start making.

"Being pretty damn sure," Forniss said, "that we haven't got anything good enough to go on. Not yet."

Heimrich sighed deeply. From without—from two tables away, which was the nearest table occupied—they were two frustrated men, met for a wake.

"Told him about the mistake somebody made in stealing a design that had nothing to do with anything?" Heimrich asked, in a voice just audible to Forniss. Forniss nodded. "Anything in yet from L.A.?" Heimrich asked. "From official sources?" Forniss said, "Nope."

The bar telephone rang shrilly. Neither Heimrich nor Forniss looked up. "Call for you, captain," Harold said, across the room. Heimrich looked at Forniss, shook his head, shrugged. He went across the room to the telephone at the end of the bar and said, "Heimrich," into it. He listened for a moment. He said, "Well, if you—" and stopped momentarily. "I can hear *you* all right," he said. "But O.K. I will." He raised his voice on that and then listened again.

"No," he said, then, and spoke even more loudly. "Hear me all right now?" He got, it appeared, an answer. "All right," he said, in the same carrying voice. "No, I can't say we have. There are a couple—" Apparently, he was interrupted. He listened again. "Twenty-four more hours?" he said and then, after another pause. "No, I can't promise anything. There's one puzzling point and something might come—" Again he was interrupted. This time he listened for some seconds.

"I don't," he said then, "say you aren't right. But I don't like to drop—"

He seemed then, for the first time, to realize that his voice was carrying through the taproom. He looked quickly, a little sheepishly, around the room. People listened.

"Look," he said, in a somewhat lowered voice. "I don't want to go into it on the phone. Suppose the sergeant and I come over and—" He stopped. "O.K.," he said, after a moment, and his voice had a weary tone. "O.K., you can listen, anyway. If we come—"

Whoever had called Heimrich was an impatient caller. Anybody in the taproom could guess that, since he so often interrupted Heimrich.

"All right," Heimrich said. "Ten's all right. Just hold it open until then. Give us a chance?" He listened again. "Naturally," Captain Heimrich said, and put the receiver back and walked slowly, heavily, back to his table.

"The D.A.," he said to Forniss, and still—no doubt forgetfully—spoke somewhat loudly. "The D.A.'s about ready to call it off. Talk to us if we go over there to Carmel, but I don't—" He, evidently, again became conscious of his raised voice and again lowered it.

They finished their drinks. They got up and walked across the taproom, two large and baffled men, and across the lounge into the dining room. One of the reporters followed them, came to their table. He couldn't, he said, help overhearing. Was he to take it that—

"Take it any way you want," Heimrich said, glumly. "I haven't any statement."

The reporter went away; carried news back to the pack.

Heimrich and Forniss waited for food; when it came, ate slowly and steadily, their attitudes discouraging approach. They were not approached—not by reporters; not by Dale, who came in alone to eat, and was joined by Latham and Chris Waggoner. Some time later, Zersk and Marley came in together. They stopped at Dale's table and there was brief colloquy. During it, Zersk looked quickly at Heimrich and Forniss and as quickly away again.

"Getting a fill-in," Heimrich said, his voice a mumble.

It was a little after eight when Heimrich and Forniss left the Inn and went out to Heimrich's car. The sun—the daylight saving sun—was preparing to set. Heimrich turned the car south on Van Brunt Avenue, which is NY-11F. Near the Bear Mountain Bridge, 11F intersects U.S. 6, which will take a car to Carmel, Putnam County seat, the lair of Putnam County's district attorney, who would have been surprised to learn the apparent extent of his influence on the New York State Police.

"I suppose it's worth while going round Robin Hood's barn," Forniss said. He was told that the night, he must remember, has a thousand eyes. They turned left on U.S. 6 and drove slowly for a few miles—drove east. At the intersection of NY-11 they turned north, which is not the way to Carmel. They drove slowly, killing daylight. It was dusk when they turned left on NY-109, which took them back toward Van Brunt. It was almost dark—which helped—when they crossed 11F at The Corners, and continued west toward the Hudson.

"I hope," Forniss said, as they turned right on Van Brunt Pass, "that we weren't too damned convincing. On account of, if they—whoever it is—thinks we're as far up the creek as you sounded like, they might just decide to leave us there. Feeling safe."

"The 'one puzzling point' ought to take care of that," Heimrich said. "Oh, I grant the risk, Charlie. But he can't afford to be complacent. If there's a puzzling point to clear up, he'll want to clear it. I would in his shoes."

Forniss supposed so. He hoped so. He said, "He?"

"Now Charlie," Heimrich said. "I think so. Which still leaves us quite a choice, naturally. You gave Mr. Fielding the same—pitch?"

"Yep. I don't know if I was quite as—thorough, as you were."

"When among actors, do as actors do," Heimrich said. "Crowley knows what to do?"

"Yep," Forniss said, and paused, since he was about, inferentially, to criticize. "I hope our client doesn't double-cross us," he said.

"God knows, so do I," Heimrich said, in a tone which caused Sergeant Forniss to regret that he had, once again, brought the subject up. "We've got to take the most likely. Take that chance."

"Crowley's a good boy," Forniss said. "And there's always the dog. Scary-looking dog."

"There's always Colonel," Heimrich agreed. "This ought to do." They were on Sugar Creek Lane by then, headed again toward the river. Heimrich nosed the car off the road, on faint tracks which led to a gap in a stone fence. When the car was well into the field beyond, not noticeable from the road, they got out.

There was still light in the western sky, but it was dark enough. They walked on up Sugar Creek Lane, hugging shadows. Ten o'clock was the most likely time, but a man with an important job to do—such as saving his own life, for example—may grow impatient.

***

Not to show himself until, and unless, he had cause; not to do anything until he had something very definite to do. Those were the instructions. The chances were a hundred to one that he would have no need to do anything. That was the prediction. The prediction came from a source in which Trooper Raymond Crowley had great trust. He himself was, Crowley realized, merely an added precaution. He parked his car as inconspicuously as he could on the edge of High Road and cut across lots, and crawled under a barbed-wire fence.

He was any hatless, reasonably good-looking, notably muscular young man taking a walk—although perhaps a somewhat peculiar walk—on a summer's evening. (A warm and sticky summer's evening.) He wore slacks and a jacket, the latter because a jacket covers a gun in a shoulder holster, not because he needed a jacket for warmth.

There was no reason to let Mrs. Faye know she was being protected. It would merely worry her needlessly, since there was almost certainly no danger. Instructions had been explicit.

Stay in some convenient shadow, close enough to the door of the house so that he could reach it quickly, if he needed to. No reason to worry about the back of the house, because there was only one door there, and a door never used, and always bolted. The bolt probably was rusted in. But Crowley knew the layout; he had been there before.

Just beyond the terrace, at the slope down from it toward the west, would be the best spot. The shadow of a big maple would be deep there, and there was not, in any case, much light on this humid, hazy night. He could see the house clearly, and could get to it quickly across the terrace—if he needed to, which he wouldn't.

He circled the house, keeping out of sight. He went a little distance down the slope and rounded the house and reached the place he had decided on. The slope there was a little steeper than he remembered it, which didn't matter. Trooper Crowley watched the house as dusk gave way to darkness; watched lights come on; could see Susan Faye moving inside. She was wearing shorts and a halter, and he felt himself a Peeping Tom. Far from any other house, Mrs. Faye would feel safe from eyes, and would have a right to. He violated her right. Nothing to be done about that, of course. Follow instructions.

He got there a little after nine. It was a few minutes after ten when Susan opened the door of the house and said, clearly, "Don't be all night about it," and let Colonel out, and closed the door after him.

The great dog stood and sniffed the air at the far edge of the terrace—stood for some seconds so and then gave a great and exuberant bound forward. Colonel knew a friend when he smelled one.

***

Their eyes adjusted, as even human eyes adjust, to the fading light. But still, they almost missed the start of the steep path—went past it once and as far as the driveway to the house; retraced their steps. Heimrich used a pencil flashlight then, unwillingly; guarded even its tiny beam with a cupped hand.

The path went straight up, was faint trail more than path. It occurred to Heimrich, leading, that scrambling deer might have made it first. He scrambled himself, clutched at trees and saplings to pull himself forward; had to continue, at intervals, to use the pencil flashlight. Perhaps, he thought, halfway up, hearing Forniss scrambling heavily behind him, it would have been better to have used the drive. Except that, using it, they could not have avoided coming out in plain sight at the top, on the turnaround.

There was light so that anyone who might be watching could see them. It was the milky light of a hazy summer's night, partly the light from stars, a little the light from the moon's slender curve. When they reached the top of the path, at some little distance from the Collins house, the house loomed unexpectedly large in the milky light. And the glass of the house darkly reflected light. There was a just perceptible sheen to the house.

Heimrich stopped and Forniss came up beside him. They stood in rough-mowed grass and looked at the house. There was no sign that anybody was in the house; no light in the house, no car in the turnaround. There was something in the open garage; something glinted there, faintly. That would, almost certainly, be the jeep. They waited; looked and listened.

Nothing moved in the house or, if there, moved in darkness.

Which seemed improbable. There was no sound. Then, far away, a dog barked; then, on the New York Central tracks far below, along the river, a diesel snorted in the night. And there was honeysuckle somewhere.

"Looks like we got here first," Forniss said, his voice just above a whisper. "Or," he added, "nobody's coming."

"Now Charlie," Heimrich said. "Somebody ought to come."

He led the way, not using the little flashlight any longer here on the hilltop, toward the looming house. If somebody was in the house, had been watching the head of the path for just such an arrival as theirs, nothing could be done about it. They circled the kitchen wing, avoiding the entrance terrace, the glass wall of the living room. They found the small door to the studio, and Heimrich used the key.

Inside the darkness was deeper; just inside, Heimrich stopped and momentarily held his breath and listened. There was the soft humming of the air-conditioning mechanism. And somewhere a faucet dripped. Some time, Heimrich thought, modern science, so intent on sending lonely objects into space, might concentrate on achieving a faucet that didn't drip. He used the little flash. A needle of light roamed the room.

It touched the pictured beauty of the dead girl, and the naked body momentarily seemed to glow with life, seemed to move as the needle of light moved. The light searched through the room, found nothing in the room.

"I suppose," Forniss said, in a voice not quite as low as before, but low still, "I suppose we'll have to leave a door unlocked. This? Or the front door? And won't anybody who comes think that's a little strange?"

"Possibly," Heimrich said. "A chance we have to take, Charlie. Maybe he'll just think luck's with him. And—we'll hear, won't we? And if he runs—"

He did not finish, but, using the flashlight sparingly, led the way out of the studio, down the corridor with sliding bedroom doors on one side, the kitchen finally on the other, and turned right into the living room. It was lighter there. Light seeped in through the glass walls, the glass door. Beyond the glass panels the water of the swimming pool was a black mirror, dimly reflecting a tree beyond the side terrace. The glass panels which separated the pool from the terrace were closed.

Beside the door there were the tumblers of two light switches in a panel. One of them, it was to be assumed—was to be hoped—controlled the floodlight over the garage door. So if someone got suspicious and ran—ran in the right place, of course—the floodlight would reveal him. If one of these switches did control it. There was no way to find out. The one for whom the trap was set might now be approaching it. Nobody walks into a trap which suddenly glares with light.

Heimrich turned the knob of the front door, releasing the lock. A trap is no good if the quarry can't get into it. He opened the door slightly and listened to the night. He motioned to Forniss, who came closer, listened too. From some distance, but evidently approaching, there was the irregular putting of a gasoline motor.

"Scooter, apparently," Heimrich said.

The sound continued to approach. It was impossible to do more than guess where the scooter, if it was the scooter, had got to when the sound stopped.

Heimrich closed the door.

"Company," he said, softly, with satisfaction. "The studio's yours, Charlie."

Forniss went across the living room, past the free-standing fireplace, through the door to the corridor, to the studio.

The living room was a difficult place to hide in, with glass on two sides and part of the third. Heimrich is a large man to hide anywhere. He went to the far side of the fireplace and crouched, so that he could look over it.

After several minutes, he saw the light from a flash. Somebody was coming up the driveway; coming, obviously, on foot. The light went out. Someone was using proper caution. It went on for an instant, and off again.

The light was closer to the ground than Heimrich had expected, and he felt a faint disquiet. Of course, the hand which held the light might be at a straightened arm's length below shoulder, which would explain that. But most people who use a flashlight carry it with the arm crooked, near waist level.

The light did not go on again. Heimrich urged his eyes; narrowed them a little, which sometimes helps. They told him nothing.

The quarry, if quarry and not some idly curious boy or girl, was cautious, had stopped to scout. Merely from caution? Or—an automobile cannot easily be hidden. Had theirs been spotted?

***

Colonel's friend wouldn't play any more. Colonel couldn't understand it. Things had started out so well, and he, refreshed by the comparative coolness of the night, had felt so much like playing. For once, it had seemed to Colonel that the curse under which he lived had been lifted—a friend had come, and offered play. It had been, for a few moments, almost as if the little god had been returned to him.

Colonel bellied down on the grass, his hind legs doubled under him; his forelegs stretched out and his great head on massive paws. His head was near his friend's head, and he whimpered softly, anxiously; invited the resumption of the game.

The friend, who lay comfortably on the grass, head pillowed on a small outcropping of rock, did not respond. Colonel whimpered further, and then sighed deeply. Things like this were always happening to him, most unfortunate of dogs. Into his large, if cloudy, mind there intruded something which may have been, formlessly, the concept of unfairness.

The friend had invited play. When Colonel bounded across the terrace toward him, the friend had raised inviting hands. When Colonel, entranced by this reception, had reared high, put great paws on welcoming shoulders, the friend had said Colonel's name—which Colonel knew very well—and then, in a different tone, something which Colonel did not understand. ("What the—" it had been, and stopped there.) The friend had moved backward under Colonel's paws, and Colonel's weight, and then had fallen backward and lain full length on the ground with his head on the outcrop of rock.

This was, Colonel had supposed, part of the game. It was, to be sure, a new game. The usual game was a brief and friendly wrestling match, with some pretended growling, with human hands clutching canine shoulders and shaking; with, eventually, all four canine feet on the ground again, and the delicious moments of waiting for something to be thrown. (Something to be fetched, if Colonel happened to remember. He is a little inclined to forget, en route, where he is going and why.)

The game did not include the friend's lying motionless, breathing harshly. Colonel had nuzzled the friend at first, trying to explain that this was not the way the game was played.

It was only after some minutes of this, and still no response to this, that Colonel had bellied down beside his friend and whimpered incomprehension into unresponsive ears. "What do you want me to do so that we can play again?" Colonel's whimper asked.

It was when he was not answered, after repeated questions, that Colonel sighed. His luck had run out again. It was no more than he expected, of course. It was the way things always happened.

XII

HEIMRICH COULD ONLY crouch behind the free-standing fireplace and look over it—keep his eyes open, keep his eyes strained, wait out the cautious visitor. He could keep ears open, too; ears strained, too. But there was little likelihood he would hear anything as long as the visitor stayed outside. The glass walls were thick and tight; the air-conditioning unit hummed gently through the house.

The visitor might do several things. If for some reason—perhaps the inadequately concealed car—he had grown suspicious, the visitor might merely go away. And with the door closed, Heimrich could not hope to hear the putt-putt of eventual departure. The visitor—the quarry, it was to be hoped; warily approaching, it was to be hoped, the trap—might decide that all was well and cross the turn-around, just beyond which it could be assumed he now lurked, and walk into Heimrich's waiting hands. He might, alternatively, edge around the house, staying out of sight—which would not be too difficult—and try the door into the studio. And walk into Forniss's waiting hands.

There did not seem to be anything especially wrong with it. Not yet, at any rate. If suspicion had been aroused, they had wasted time with their trap, and would have to think of something else. But it was most likely that necessity would, in the end, outweigh caution. Whoever had come up the driveway had felt compelled to come, to chance it. The same compulsion, which must be extreme, might be expected to continue to dominate. I hope, Heimrich thought to himself, and crouched and waited, and watched for movement in the night. He waited for some minutes. He worried while he waited, worried more as he waited longer. He could not determine why, if there did not seem to be anything obviously wrong with it, there was still something obscurely wrong with it. Not the delay. The delay was reasonable. Wary animals sniff around what may prove to be a trap. A wary animal this one almost certainly was; wary and, it could hardly be denied, ingenious. Then—what? That the light had seemed closer to the ground than was to be—

It was brief and intangible; it seemed, for an instant, to be entirely in Heimrich's mind and there indecipherable. The senses had, for the flicker of an instant, responded to something. Sound? Light? *Light.* That was it. Somewhere, a flash of light.

The mind caught up with the senses. Light, briefly around him. No—*behind* him. Light without center, only a momentary pulsation in the room. Or—beyond the room?

Heimrich, not standing, turned. In the dim light, one of the glass panels between side terrace and pool was moving. He watched through intervening glass, across dark water. The panel was moving almost invisibly; it was only that, at the end most distant from him, a slit appeared in the glass wall—a slit of just perceptibly clearer night.

He waited. A flashlight had been used, briefly, to find the control button—the button rendered inconspicuous by its housing. Somebody had known where to look, and had needed to look only briefly. Now, still invisible, still outside, somebody waited to see whether the soundless opening of the glass panel was noticed, led to anything.

Heimrich tried to be as soundless as glass moving in almost frictionless channels. He did not quite manage it as he edged around the fireplace, got it between himself and the inner glass panels which separated living room from pool. But, since those panels were still closed, since the visitor—the wary intruder to the trap—was still outside, he thought he had been quiet enough. And if whoever was coming in used the flashlight to search the living room, Heimrich might be missed. Which was desirable. Let the quarry commit himself. And, it was even possible that there might be bait in a baitless trap. It would be pleasant if their visitor, looking for something which existed only in a policeman's strategy, found something more actual, and to a policeman useful.

Minutes passed, and the light was not used again. A very cautious quarry, a very worried small animal. Small? Why had he thought "Small?" The light carried low. That, of course, was it. But this animal would not be small; not if Heimrich's hunch had any validity. Not if—

The visitor was, on that instant, a black shadow in the narrow oblong of clearer night. Black—entirely black. And—*small*. Still indistinguishable; a figure all in black, with a blurred face which seemed to float above shadow. Tight black sweater, close black slacks, black sneakers—that would be the costume. Not, certainly, a costume of innocence.

The shadow moved, the deeper blackness moved. Moved beside the pool at the far end; moved quickly, with assurance, needing no light. Heimrich watched. He swore, without sound. A woman, obviously. A young woman, obviously. The movement was female movement; the sure-footed grace was youth's grace. Undoubtedly the rubber-soled sneakers made a soft padding sound on the tile of the ledge which surrounded the pool. Heimrich could not hear the sound, with the inner panels closed.

She knew where she was going, and now Heimrich also knew. She was making for the door which led to shower and dressing room between the pool and the studio. So—heading for the studio. Where Forniss waited. Waited, Heimrich was afraid, too openly. He could not think of anything in the studio which would give even as much concealment as the fireplace behind which he himself crouched. Unless Forniss could manage to hide himself behind canvas. Or, conceivably, behind the easel. His legs would show, but—

The girl went through the door, still no more than a moving

shadow, still unrecognizable. Not that there was much doubt. Reconsideration was called for. Heimrich could not argue that his hunch had included surreptitious entry by Miss Chris Waggoner, rather extremely costumed for the task. All very well here, now that she was here. But she had had to get here and must have been, on a scooter, on a warm evening, conspicuously got up for something.

The costume, certainly, was in character. Only—this was not. Never before that he could remember had Captain M. L. Heimrich found so much difficulty in making the character fit the crime. Well, he had guessed wrong, evaluated wrong.

There was no longer any sufficient reason to crouch uncomfortably behind the low pedestal of the fireplace. Heimrich started to stand up.

And as he stood, the room was flooded with light. He dropped again, but doubted whether he had been quick enough. Not if this new visitor, the headlights of whose car glared through glass into the room, had had his eyes open. And Heimrich was still on the wrong side of the fireplace. He was on the floor—full on the floor, now. Did one of the chairs partially screen him? He twisted to look. Very partially.

On the other hand, this new visitor had clearly approached with mind unwary. There was nothing surreptitious about this arrival. So, perhaps, there had been no concentration on what headlights showed.

Then, as abruptly as the room had come alive with light, it died in darkness. The headlights had been switched off. Heimrich moved around the fireplace to the far side, and looked over it, and was in time to see a large shadow get out of the car. A man, this one was. He, also, seemed to be wearing dark clothing. His face, too, was only a pale blur in milky light. He came toward the door openly enough, and reached for the glass knob. He did not seem surprised when it turned in his hand. He came into the room.

He came in and, without pause, without hesitation, rushed at Heimrich. He had some distance to come across the room; he came with reckless determination and almost absurd confidence. It was evident that he had not only seen Heimrich when the headlights picked him out, but memorized his position in the room. And planned to do something very definite about it.

The charging man's hands were empty. That much Heimrich saw, as he came up to his feet, set himself. He would hardly, in any case, have had time to draw his gun from its shoulder holster.

The big man—and now he was close enough so that Heimrich could see his face, and see it with some surprise—did not say anything. He merely ran at Heimrich, with hands formed into fists. Heimrich thought, in the instant before they met, that the man did not recognize him, although he recognized the man.

"*Hold*—" Heimrich said, loudly, and had meant to add "it" but did not have a chance.

The man was there. The man swung. Explanation, if any was available, would have to wait.

Heimrich moved, and the blow—which might well have knocked him half across the room—grazed his face.

Heimrich's answering left moved only inches, and did not graze anything. The charging man came to a halt, but swung again. Heimrich used his right, this time—used it with solid pounds behind it. And the man staggered.

"You damn—" Heimrich said, and blocked a roundhouse right. Strong and agile the man was, but not up to this sort of thing. Heimrich had always supposed that boxing was something—like dancing and, presumably, riding horses—that all actors had to learn. Apparently not, Heimrich decided, and, with some reluctance, knocked George Latham sprawling on the tile floor. He slid on the floor. He slid into a table and knocked it over.

Physical combat is a hazard of the policeman's trade. Heimrich, like most policemen, was prepared for it. It was a little hard on the knuckles.

"Now Mr. Latham," Heimrich said, as Latham began to scramble to his feet, set himself to charge again. "What on earth is all this—"

Latham put his hands down. (Then he raised one of them to rub his jaw.) He said, *"You?"* loudly, in a tone of complete astonishment. "What are you doing here?"

"Working," Heimrich said. "And what are—"

He did not finish. Feet pounded in the corridor, pounded down from the studio. Forniss to the rescue, Forniss to join in. The table had banged loudly on the tile floor. Latham had not fallen silently. But Forniss wouldn't leave the—

Forniss came into the room with his gun ready. He stopped abruptly.

"You won't need it, Charlie," Heimrich said. "Mr. Latham isn't —*where's the girl, Charlie?*"

And Charles Forniss looked at him blankly. Forniss repeated, "Girl?"

"She *is* here," Latham said, and yelled it. "Where is she? What's happened to—"

"Get back," Heimrich said, to Forniss. "She's probably there by now, even if she—"

Forniss did not wait. He went. Latham clenched his fists again, confronted Heimrich again.

"If anything—" he shouted.

"Shut up," Heimrich said. "Quit yelling. Go with Forniss."

Heimrich himself ran to the glass paneling between pool and living room. He did not wait to see if Latham went as he was told. He wasted moments finding the handhold hollowed in the glass. Then he slid the panel open violently and ran on slippery tile—it would be a fine ending to this confused affair if he fell into the pool—toward the door which opened on the dressing room. His shoes clattered on the tile. But there was no longer any use in silence.

Heimrich and Forniss confronted each other at opposite ends of a narrow room, with a shower stall in one corner, a dressing table along one wall. There was nothing else between them. There was no black-clad girl in the room. Latham appeared behind Forniss and demanded, in a shout, to be told where Chris was.

It took only moments to find out, not where she was, but how she had got away from where they were. She had not bothered, not taken time, to close the studio door behind her. The shadow of Chris Waggoner had rejoined other shadows of the night.

Heimrich had run halfway down the driveway toward the road, and Forniss had had time to scramble some distance down the path, before they heard the putt-putt of the scooter. They were too distant to consult, and did not need to. They plodded back and met on the turnaround, by the Buick station wagon in which George Latham had precipitously arrived. Latham was getting into it.

"Now Mr. Latham," Heimrich said, and took his arm. Latham got out of the Buick. He whirled as he backed out of it, wrenched his arm free. He faced Heimrich then, glared at him—a large and solid and very angry young man. His fists doubled.

"Now Mr. Latham," Heimrich said, mildly. "Do we have to go through that again?"

The glare faded from Latham's face, faded slowly, left behind it an expression of anxiety. (What mobile faces these actors have, Heimrich thought.)

"Suppose," Heimrich said, "you tell me what this is all about, Mr. Latham."

Latham made a quick gesture, as if he would relegate that to some other time.

"You're going to stand here?" he said. "Talk? Not try to find out what's happening to Chris?"

"She's going somewhere on the scooter," Heimrich said. "Probably back to the Center, to the Inn. She'll be all—"

"How the hell do you know she will?" Latham said.

The answer was obvious.

"Why shouldn't she be?"

"Because," Latham said, "can't you see—she's trying to find something. This—this thing you were hinting about. Whatever it was that somebody was after and got the design by mistake for. For God's sake, man!"

"She told you that? Did she tell you what she expected to find?"

Latham made the gesture again.

"You're wasting time," Heimrich said. "She told you she was coming here? To—*find something she'd missed before?* Something she couldn't let us find?"

"For God's sake," Latham said. "Not that *she'd* left. Something that would prove what she guessed."

"Which was?"

Latham shook his head slowly.

"I don't know," he said, and his voice was suddenly dull. "She wouldn't tell me. Said it was only a guess."

"But, that she was coming here? To look?"

Latham shook his head again. He said he hadn't known about that. He said "the damn fool kid," and there was anxiety in his voice; more than anxiety. (In his actor's voice.)

"You'll just stand here?" he said. "Do nothing? Until—until I go through the whole thing?"

"Now Mr. Latham," Heimrich said, and meant "yes" and was so understood.

Then—

There had been nothing tangible, George Latham told them. Chris Waggoner had seemed, to him, abstracted. "As if she had something in that mind of hers." He had tried to find out what; been told that it had nothing to do with him; told that he would learn soon enough.

"This," Heimrich said, "was after I had a telephone conversation? That a good many of you overheard?"

Latham looked at him through abruptly narrowed eyes. He said, slowly, that he'd be damned. He also said that he ought to have known, that they all ought to have known. Heimrich merely waited.

It had been after that, after dinner, that Latham had found the girl abstracted, as if she were "up to something." Or, about to be. "I know that crazy little mind of hers," Latham said, and, paradoxically, his tone was one of admiration. He had tried to find out what the thing, the plan, in her mind was. He had been told only that he would find out in time and—"that she was pretty sure of something." That was what she had said. He had tried to get her to promise not to do anything, barge into anything, and had been told not to play the heavy. And then that she was tired, and that he bored her, and that she was going to bed.

Latham, annoyed—and himself tired and hot—had had a nightcap in the taproom and gone up to his own room, on the second floor. It was a room that looked out over the parking lot. He had stripped down to shorts, and sat near the window and smoked, and wished he were cooler, and that the crazy kid weren't so much under his skin. Or so, now, he said.

He had not seen Chris cross the parking lot. He had not been looking. It was when he heard the scooter start up that he looked.

"And there she was," he said. "In the silliest damn getup I ever saw—black sweater. On a night like this. Black slacks. Wonder is she wasn't wearing a mask and—and carrying a magnifying glass. The crazy little—made up like something in a scare movie. The crazy—"

"You saw her in the parking lot light, I suppose."

Latham merely nodded to the obvious.

"What I'm getting at," he said. "She might as well—have carried a sign. In lights. 'I'm up to something. I'm the girl detective.'" He moved abruptly, as if to get back into the car. He stopped before he was stopped.

"Don't you get it?" he asked, his tone now weary. "Anybody could have seen her. Anybody. Whoever it was she was trying to get something on. And—" He shrugged his shoulders, hopelessly. "We just stand here," he said.

"Mr. Latham," Heimrich said. "Hasn't it really occurred to you that you may have things upside down? That she planned things that way? That she herself—"

"Damn it," Latham said. "*No*, damn it!" His denial was violent.

And Latham could not, Heimrich thought, more clearly have disclosed his own uneasiness, his own doubt. Heimrich looked at Latham; saw realization of this in Latham's face. (His actor's face. It is an actor's profession to reveal. To reveal what is chosen to be revealed. Which was, of course, the catch—the catch in so much of this.)

"So," Heimrich said, "you decided to follow her. To—protect her."

"And a hell of a lot of good I've been," Latham said. "Am being now. But—you can call it that."

He had dressed quickly, putting on whatever was close to hand. Heimrich looked at the man in the dark blue polo shirt, the dark gray slacks, the black shoes. Not as obviously, not as theatrically, he, too, was dressed to move unnoticed through the night.

Latham looked puzzled. Then he said, "Oh, I see what you mean. It just happened."

He was told to go on. He said there wasn't much more. He had dressed and gone downstairs and out of the Inn—

"See anybody you knew?"

He hadn't. He hadn't been looking for anybody. He might have been seen, if that was what Heimrich was getting at.

[165]

"Go on, Mr. Latham."

He had assumed the station wagon would be unlocked. It almost always was. It had been. So—

"So you came here," Heimrich said. "Guessing that she would come here."

"Hell," Latham said. "You made it plain enough."

"And," Heimrich said, "jumped me. Very—impetuously. Thinking?"

"All I saw was—somebody," Latham said. "Anybody. Thought whoever it was—whoever Chris suspected—had got here ahead of her and was waiting for her."

"Who?" Heimrich said, and was looked at blankly. "Did you think I might be?"

Latham shrugged. He hadn't had a notion.

"Somebody my size?"

But even that did not help. Until Heimrich had stood up—"and got ready to knock me down"—Latham had not, he said, had any idea as to the man's size. His glimpse in the headlights had been brief; Heimrich had not been standing. As far as that went, he might have been—anybody.

Such as?

If he wanted names, Latham couldn't guess at names. If Heimrich couldn't. All right, then—Marley, Dale, "this fellow Fielding." All about the right size. Zersk—Zersk was smaller, sure. But, again, until he was in the room, already "trying to knock somebody's block off," Latham had had no clear idea of the size of the man he had seen.

"Looks to me," Latham said, "as if you didn't catch what you wanted in this trap of yours. Unless—" He stopped suddenly, as if the idea had just then entered his mind. "For God's sake," he said. "You don't think it was me?"

"Now Mr. Latham."

"Assume it isn't me," Latham said. "Assume Collins didn't kill

Peggy and himself. Somebody's wandering around who's killed two people. Only—*not wandering now, is he?* Not wandering into this trap of yours, anyway. And—if I noticed Chris was planning something, anybody might have noticed. And the crazy kid is off somewhere on that damned scooter—"

There was, obviously, something to what Latham said. And—there was more to it.

Young Crowley was there. Crowley was competent to take care of things. Nothing could slip up. Only—

"Stick around," Heimrich told Latham, told Forniss—the latter with a nod at Latham. "I want to make a telephone call."

XIII

THE GOOFY DOG was taking his own sweet time about it. Which was like him; which was one of the things that made him a goofy dog. Probably he had forgotten what he had gone out to do and had found a place where the grass was cool and lain down on it and gone to sleep on it. When she finished the chapter, she would go out and call him.

Not that that would necessarily do any good. Young Michael—when young Michael called it was different. Colonel came then, a lumbering Lassie. When she herself called, anything was likely to happen—a distant bark, a rush of great dog (or an amble of same) or nothing whatever. Which was another thing which made Colonel such a goofy dog. Susan had tried to put herself in Colonel's place—more difficult, she found, than to put herself in the place of a more average dog—and decide why he behaved so. It seemed to be generally true that the greater distance away he was the more likely he was to respond to a call. (Which made no particular sense to Susan, pretending to be a dog named Colonel.) If he was near by, he was more likely to make no response at all. This, Susan thought, might be due to the fact that, in his hazy mind, Colonel considered himself already there—or, probably, "here." "Here, Colonel." But in Colonel's mind, he was. That might account for it.

Susan sat under a light, with a book, in shorts and minimal strapless halter. She wore even so much because, probably, she would have to go out and wander around in search of Colonel. Not that anybody would see her if she wandered naked—which on a night such as this would be most sensible—but still— Country, as somebody had said, is where you don't have to pull the shades. But still—

Given time, of course, Colonel would return of his own accord. He returned, often, quite abruptly, and this was particularly true at night. At a guess—Susan's guess—realization that he was alone in the dark came over him suddenly, unexpectedly, and he hurried home to light and reassurance. Sometimes he was obviously frightened—looked, as Susan told him then, no doubt unfairly, as if he had been chased by a rabbit. Susan, sitting under a light—which was hot —turned a page and, after a time, another page. She reached the end of the chapter. It was really too hot a night to sit under a lamp, try to keep one's mind on words. She would get Colonel in and turn lights off and go to bed. Or, perhaps, with Colonel secured, sit on the terrace in the milky darkness and, probably, contemplate the great oaf—the solid man who shied at phantoms. It would be cooler on the terrace.

She went to the door and opened it and called Colonel's name. She waited. Perhaps this was a responsive night. She called more loudly and nothing happened and she thought, Damn the dog, and stepped out and called again. No pony-size dog galumphed out of darkness, or straggled out. She stepped farther out on the terrace.

And a man came out of shadows onto the turnaround, gravel grating under his feet, and made a motion—an up-and-down motion, a silencing, warning motion, with what he carried in his hand. Pale light, drifting through the windows of the house, fell on the man, on what he carried.

Susan Faye could only gaze at him, gaze with disbelief. Because he had come not only out of the shadows of the night. He had come out of the shadows of the past.

He wore a leather jerkin, and a broad-brimmed hat of curious shape. He wore leather boots which came to mid-thigh and flared there. The hat was pulled low, so that most of his face was in shadow. Below the shadow, a pointed beard jutted.

The pistol he carried in his hand should have been an ancient flintlock. It was not.

For an instant, Susan's reeling mind told her only that this was preposterous, that this was an hallucination. But in almost the same instant, she knew that the man was quite solid, quite real, and that he was one of the men who were making the picture, and was in the costume of the picture.

She was conscious, momentarily, of relief—a ghost did not walk her terrace. Just a man, dressed up fantastically, come to—

And in that instant of realization, that at first reassuring close of the mind on the safe matter of fact, Susan shivered with fear.

Who? her mind called out. Come to—what?

The mind's time is not real time. Susan's raced from bewilderment to relief to fear while the man in the clothes the Dutch had worn along the Hudson three hundred years before took two long steps toward her, with no sound but the grating of leather bootsoles on gravel. The moving pistol spoke for him; for an instant of greater fear Susan thought that the pistol alone would speak.

"Go back in," the man said. His voice was oddly husky; it was as if he whispered loudly. It was as if something were wrong with his throat. "Turn off the light."

The gun in his hand moved, then, impatiently, as if it were more restless than the hand which held it.

Susan backed toward the door, moved slowly, her hands raised in the futile semblance of protection.

"Don't be afraid," the man said, in the same voice—the same false voice. That was it—a *false voice.* "You'll be all right if you tell me."

And, as she moved backward, groped behind her and pulled the screen open, he moved forward. But he did not lessen the distance between them.

"Just go in and turn off the light," the man said. "There'll be all the light we'll need."

She went in, went half across the room to the lamp, and, with her hand on it, turned. The man was a shadow at the door; his head was down so that, more than before, the broad brim of his archaic hat shadowed his face. Shadowed all but the beard, which was itself a shadow.

He did not move in the door, only waited. She turned the light off—the friendly light, the protecting light. With the light gone, the costumed man in the doorway disappeared for a moment—all but disappeared. Then, as her eyes adjusted, he was there again. He came into the room. He closed the screen door and then the glass-paneled front door. Now faint shadows came into the room from the night's milky glow; came through windows on either side of the door, through the glass in the door.

The faint light fell on Susan; her naked arms and legs were white in it. She said, "Who are you? What do you want?"

And as she said that she thought—*One of them has a beard.* The one with the beard! The only one she knew by sight. The one half the country knew by sight.

"You're Dale," she said. "Francis Dale. What are you doing here?"

The pistol moved impatiently; moved back and forth.

"What was wrong at the house?" the man said. He used the same hoarse, loud whisper.

"I don't know what you mean," she said. "Why do you go on talking that way?"

She felt exasperated anger that he should go on talking that way. It was amazing that annoyance over anything so trivial should, even momentarily, replace fear. But perhaps the falseness of the voice was part of the fear. She struck at it, and struck at fear.

"You know what I mean," the man said. "Something wrong. Something didn't fit the picture. What was it?" The voice did not change.

Susan's mind raced. How did he— *Of course.* The man who had

SHOW RED FOR DANGER

stood outside the window. This was the man. Francis Dale—he was the man.

"The design," she said. He knew already. "Brian had—" She hesitated. Give him more to be afraid of? Or, less? "There was a message in the design. But—you know that. You stole—"

"That's no good," the man said, and for a moment the voice was a "real" voice. Real, and impatient—and harsh with impatience. "There wasn't any message." The husky whisper came back with that. Why, since she knew who he was, had told him she knew, did he keep on with that?

"It's only," she said, "that you couldn't see it. The message—"

But the man was shaking his head, and shaking it with certainty.

"I told you that's no good," he said. "The other thing. The thing you told Heimrich you couldn't remember. You're going to remember it, aren't you? Now. For me."

"Told—" she began, and stopped again. Merton must have told him that—that there was something other than the design, something she couldn't remember. Why? *Why?* There must have been some reason—

"That's right," the man said. "Think. You'll remember. If you remember you'll be all right."

But that was a lie. She wouldn't be all right—not any way it worked out. If she had something to remember, she could not be left alive to remember. If she couldn't remember—

A kind of hopeless rage filled her. *He—he*—had done this to her. Lied, for some reason of his own. Left her—left her holding a lie which was shapeless in her hands. And—*left her to this man with a gun.* I'll never forgive him this, she thought, and then, *I'm thinking as if I'll live to.*

"There wasn't anything else," she said. "Only the design. He—he fooled you."

And me, she thought. *And me!*

"Mrs. Faye," the man said, "this isn't getting us anywhere. There was something else. I think you have remembered what it was. I think—"

She started to speak.

"Wait," he said. "It may be something quite trivial. Something of no danger to—anyone. Or, something for which there's an entirely reasonable explanation. Then—then we could all quit worrying, couldn't we?"

Think of something, Susan told herself. Think of something trivial enough, meaningless enough. Something that will get me out of this, so I can tell him how I hate him for this. Please, somebody, give me the right lines to speak. Please—

The ringing of the telephone was a shattering sound in the room. Instinctively, she turned.

"Let it ring," the man said. "Just let it ring." The gun, which seemed to have a life of its own—a sharp and savage life—lifted a little.

The telephone bell rang. She had never known it rang so loudly. It rang again and again.

"You expected somebody to call?" the man said, over the ringing, in the momentary pauses between the bell's clamor.

"No," she said and then, quickly, "Yes. I—"

And knew she had been too slow in catching honesty by the tail. He laughed. The bell kept on ringing, as if it would never stop.

She still stood by the table which held the lamp. The useless lamp. And—*a bronze figure of a crouching leopard.* A thing big Michael had seen somewhere and liked and brought home and—and *an object heavy for its size.* A thing the hand could close on.

She could not look down at it. That would give its existence away, give her hope away. Her hand dangled near it; she moved her hand. The light from the window lay across only half the table, did not lie on the crouching leopard.

She moved her hand into the shadow. He did not seem to notice this. He seemed to be looking beyond her as he waited for the telephone to stop ringing. Her fingers touched the leopard. It was cold under her fingers. She left them there. There would be a better time. There had to be a better time.

The telephone bell stopped ringing. He would concentrate again on her with the ringing over—the ringing which had, somehow, been an intermission. He must not look at her hand in the shadow. She looked at him, beyond him, as if she saw something behind him. Where there was nothing—nothing but windows and wall, and glass-paneled door. Where—

Who *had* telephoned, Susan wondered. Not that it mattered. Not now. It might have been Merton—the one who had got her into this. Calling to—to what? Make sure she was having a peaceful evening? Tell her a pleasant goodnight?

"To get back to it," the man said. "We may as well get back to it. There's no great hurry, but—"

The only chance was to make him believe the truth. Not the lie he must have been told. Why? *Why?* Heimrich must have had—

Of course. A trap. With her as bait. I'll kill that man, Susan thought. I'll get my hands on that man and— Her mind jerked to a stop.

Behind this man in leather jerkin, leather boots—this absurdly costumed menace—there was movement. Susan had been looking beyond him, her eyes unfocused. There was movement—no, had been movement. She had missed—

There was a shadow against the glass panel of the door. A shadow moved, was gone. It seemed to move downward, as if someone had been standing at the door and then had crouched below the panel.

"You saw something that you thought was wrong," the man said, patiently, explaining it all over again. "All I want you to do is to tell me what it was."

"Mr. Dale," she said, "there wasn't anything. I told you, Captain Heimrich lied to you. I don't know why. To—to make you do something, probably. Something like this. Something that would—"

"No," he said. "You overestimate him, Mrs. Faye. He isn't very bright, you know. Anybody can see he isn't very bright. He wouldn't think of anything like that. He—"

The front door opened inward. It opened then—opened behind the man—opened with sudden violence.

He had been there waiting. He—

A lithe shadow came through the door. A shadow with a white blur of face—a slight figure—a—a *girl*. A girl all in black, dark hair hanging loose.

The costumed man whirled and the girl said—cried—"I knew it would be—" and the man had her arm, was twisting her toward him.

As he turned to the girl, grabbed at the girl, he turned partly away from Susan. In that instant, Susan threw the bronze leopard —threw it with all the strength of a tennis-hardened right arm, and threw it at the man's head.

And—missed his head. But the little statue, so heavy for its size, hit his right shoulder and must, for a moment, have numbed the hand which held the gun. Because as he turned back toward Susan, and released the black-clad girl, the gun dropped to the floor.

The girl spun away, off balance. And Susan ran toward the man, toward the gun on the floor—crouched and threw herself down for it in a kind of dive.

The man clutched at her. His fingers slipped from her bare shoulder. But they caught in the elastic inset of the strapless halter and the halter pulled away and down and his fingers slipped from it.

Some reflexes are fatal, some betray. Without realizing what she did—then realizing too late—Susan used the hand which might, which just might, have reached the gun to clutch at the slipping halter, pull it back where it belonged, cover breasts with it. And, as the man kicked the gun from her reach, Susan made a shuddering sound, half a sob, of realization—of the realization of utter, reflexive —*idiocy*. The man used his left hand then to hurl her back, and she went down in a sitting posture and slid helplessly on the floor. And the man picked the gun up.

He moved the gun back and forth, pointing at the girl in black, at Susan. They shared the gun; the gun instructed. They moved as the gun ordered, stood side by side—a slender girl absurdly in black; the taller woman in brief shorts and briefer halter. But halter in the right place, now; modesty restored, now.

And Susan, standing, looking at the man, half seeing him, raged at herself—raged at all the idiocy, the reflexive responsiveness, which had somehow (without her knowing, without her willing) been built into her. Die, but die modest. Be killed, but keep covered.

There ought to be dignity, her mind screamed at her. It shouldn't be—funny, grotesque! So that your mind screamed with hating laughter at itself, while it drew back in fear.

"You wouldn't have got it anyway," the girl beside her said, in a voice that, curiously, vibrated. "He's very strong. Too strong." It was oddly as if she read lines. "And evil," the girl said, in the same voice, but more or less, it seemed, as an afterthought. And then, in an entirely different voice, a child's pleased voice, she said, "Anyway, I got his beard."

And she held out, in long and slender fingers, a neatly pointed beard.

"It was like you to wear the beard," the child said, in the other voice, with dark contempt. "*So* like you."

But then—not Francis Dale? Because—but why had she been sure Dale's beard was real? Why—of course! He had worn the beard when she had pointed him out to young Michael, had said to the boy, "That's Francis Dale." But then Dale had not been in costume, had been wearing polo shirt and slacks. The beard was part of costume. Then—

"But—who?" Susan Faye said, and the girl beside her said, "But of course—"

The man said, loudly, "Be quiet, Chris! Shut up, Chris!"

The gun added to the order. The girl stopped.

The man looked at them, back still to light, face still shadowed by the grotesque hat. But I wouldn't know him anyway, Susan thought. All I know about them—except that I saw Dale once or twice and knew him—all I know is what *he* told me. And she thought of the man she meant when she thought "he" and there was a kind of curdling inside her, a welling sourness.

"As for wearing the beard," the man said. "I wanted to give her a chance, Chris. Only, I'm afraid you've loused it up, haven't you? With your—play acting. Because now, obviously, I've got to do something about you and—" He shrugged the shoulders under the leather jerkin.

"The reason for all this," he said and, with his free hand, indicated jerkin, leather boots. "Give her a chance to tell and not know who she told. See, Chris?"

"You'd have done it anyway," Chris Waggoner said, and now, again, spoke in the lower voice, the voice which vibrated—vibrated again with contempt.

The crazy kid, Susan thought. Doesn't she—*realize?* And then her mind was suddenly dark, groping. Do I?

"Not without reason," the man said. But now he did not speak in the assumed voice; it was as if, with the falseness of the beard snatched away, he had had himself stripped away the other falseness. As no longer sustainable? No—more than that. As no longer *necessary*. Which meant—

It was harshly clear what it meant. And the incongruity, the almost farcical element, remained. Because the voice this costumed man now used was one which Susan had never heard before. Disguising it had been the theatrical device, meaningless. To die in the midst of costumed farce! There ought to be dignity—

"Never without reason," the man said, in the deep voice, the unknown voice.

"Moth—" Chris began and the man said, "Be quiet, you little fool!" And then he sighed, as if in deep regret.

"Determined, aren't you?" he said. "Determined to get the lady killed. Because—"

And then he stopped, half turned. Susan moved, but the gun moved more quickly, pointed with finality, and she stopped. She looked again toward the door, open now, only a screen between the room and night.

There was no movement. But something had distracted, disturbed, the costumed man. She listened. She heard nothing.

***

Fifty yards from the house, beyond the terrace, hidden because there the ground pitched down, Colonel had gone to sleep beside the friend who refused to play. He had heard dimly, as in a dream—even when awake he heard most things as in a dream—the familiar voice of the one who lived with the little god. She had been calling him. But he was already there. He whimpered briefly to his friend and, getting nothing for his trouble, went back to sleep. It was some time before he was again awakened.

A sharp sound awakened him. (It was the sound of metal against wood as a gun dropped; to Colonel only a harsh and unaccustomed sound.) He moved his ears first, focusing on the sound. It was not repeated, but he heard other sounds and raised his head and turned it. People making their sounds. He listened. Not the sound that was important, not the little god. So—

He looked at the unresponsive friend. He reached forward and, wetly, licked the face.

And Trooper Raymond Crowley, who also had been dreaming vaguely, came awake. He came awake with a headache, at first with fog in his mind, then with sharp awareness which turned into alarm, anxiety. He remembered it clearly enough—the big dog leaping at him playfully, putting paws on shoulders; the loss of footing on the sloping turf, the effort to catch himself, the failure. Hit his head on something, obviously. Knocked himself out, obviously. But— *How long ago?*

He stood up and for a moment was dizzy. He fought the dizziness away. He looked across the terrace toward the house. It was dark. But on either side of the doorway a man stood—each a shape only, a dark shadow outlined against the lighter background of the house.

Crowley got his gun out. The men had only to look across the terrace to see him. They did not seem to be looking across the terrace. Crowley crouched and began to work his way around the terrace. The slope of the ground helped. Circle the terrace, get between the lurking men—why *two* men?—and their car, then close in.

Colonel sat up, interested. The game was on again. Not the usual game. Still—

Colonel followed his moving friend. Crowley swore silently. All he needed now, was this stupid great dog, who would be likely to bark at any time. Who would surely bark if spoken to, told to get the hell out of there; told to find a good place for it and drop dead.

There was a panel truck at the bottom of the drive. It was an outline in the dim light. Near it was another man—the shadow of another man. He would have to be got first. If Crowley could get up behind him, crouch in the shadows of bushes, use the gun as a hammer—

***

[179]

There wasn't anything to hear. There wasn't anybody coming. This was it. We've had it. Face it—bring truth and dignity back to this farcical charade.

"You killed them," Susan Faye told the costumed man. Her voice was steady. "Killed her. Then Brian. To make his look like suicide. I don't know who you are. But you killed them."

He merely looked at her.

"It's you who're the fool," she said. "A silly, dressed-up fool. A—"

The girl came to her, then, the gun ignored. The girl clung to her. "Don't let him," the girl said, and the voice was a child's voice— the voice of a terrified child. "Don't let Paul—"

Susan put an arm around the trembling child.

"There," Susan said. "There, Chris. He won't. He's done, now—all done. Washed-up. He's had it, Chris."

And that wasn't true. It was the other way around—all the other way. But face it; bring dignity to it.

"He can't get away with it again," Susan said.

"Why?" the man said, as if he were interested. "It worked before. I got away with it before."

"You didn't. That's the whole—"

"When they find you," the man said. "And the gun in Chris's hand. That will be enough. They swallowed the other until you found—whatever it was you found. Coat it enough, they'll swallow anything. I learned that on the Coast. And what you found doesn't matter now, does it? Because—"

He whirled at the sound, and was almost quick enough. He got one shot off as the two men came through the door, and George Latham made a grunting sound but kept on coming. It was Heimrich, trained for that sort of thing, who knocked the gun from Paul Marley's hand before he could fire again, and then knocked Marley off his feet.

Marley lay on the floor and looked up at Heimrich.

"Thanks for telling us," Heimrich said.

Chris Waggoner said, "Oh. *Oh!*" and was out of Susan's protecting arm, running toward George Latham.

"He *hit* you!" she said. "Hurt you. I'll—I'll kill him. George. *George.*"

There was blood dripping, but barely dripping, from the side of George Latham's head. He held the dark-haired girl close, made soothing sounds to her.

"You're brave," the girl said, in her deeper voice. "*So* brave."

Susan Faye stood unmoving and, for all the shimmering whiteness of her arms and legs and shoulders it was as if she drew a cloak around her, a dark cloak.

She looked at Heimrich; looked long at him. Then she turned and walked away from all of them—walked the length of the room and into her bedroom. She closed the door of the bedroom and, in the sudden silence, all of them could hear the click of the lock as she turned the key.

XIV

HEIMRICH HAD GOT to bed at a little after six in the morning, and told himself that tomorrow was another day—had to be another day. He slept; he has learned to sleep when he can. But he dreamed—dreamed of eyes which were cold, unseeing. It is not usual for him to dream. He called Susan Faye for the first time at eight-thirty in the morning. She hung up as soon as she heard his voice.

Heimrich looked at the telephone and swore at it—swore wearily. He was very tired; it had taken almost all the night. He had driven back from Carmel in the morning's daylight, and should have been satisfied. Confronted with it at a little after three in the morning, Paul Marley—kept awake and waiting for some hours; given ample time to worry—had, after it was laid out for him, said, "O.K. Now for God's sake leave me alone," and then, rather unexpectedly, "It was a lousy trick you played, captain." Which was a strange moral judgment from a man who had killed three people and planned to kill two more.

The district attorney, like Heimrich himself, was convinced that Marley would, worked on enough, be more communicative. Not that it mattered particularly. He had been communicative enough, explicit enough, in the hearing of four people—two women he had a gun on, two men who waited and listened outside a screen door. A full and signed confession is always a convenient thing to have, but would hardly, in this instance, be necessary. They had enough.

Aside from the most immediate thing—that Paul Marley had walked into a set trap and, being in it, unknowingly squealed, as trapped things do—they had had rather more by the time Heimrich drove through the night from Van Brunt Center to Carmel, the county seat, where Marley was locked up, waiting.

It did not matter that they were still some distance from proving that Paul Marley had begun his killings—his killings staged as suicide—by killing his wife.

"I *know* he did," Chris Waggoner said. "I think I always knew it." She used her deeper voice for that. George Latham was sitting beside her, a brief bandage on his scratched head. He held her hand. Heimrich was not sure, but he thought the tall young man—the "brave" young man, a judgment with which Captain Heimrich had no reason to quarrel—pressed the hand he held. At any rate, she said, "All right, George," in her younger voice, and in a tone of contentment—of contented trust. (Which had given Merton Heimrich occasion to wince, and again to see cold eyes, hear a lock click.)

Chris had had only belief, as Heimrich, when he first listened to Forniss's report from the Coast, had had only a hunch. He had a little more now. One Dr.—the appellation belonged, it was evident, in quotation marks—Robert Wiley had, pressed, admitted acceptance of a somewhat irregular fee. For value received, he had agreed, eighteen months before, to say that Mrs. Gertrude Marley, formerly Mrs. Gertrude Waggoner, had been given treatments by him, and had been in a depression. The fee had been proffered in Paul Marley's name.

"Dr." Wiley had defended himself, rather weakly. He had said that she might well have been; that most people he ran into in Hollywood were, from time to time. And he had no reason to suspect that Marley had had anything to do with his wife's death, and didn't now, and that he had done it to make things easier all around for everybody. The Hollywood police had, fortuitously, questioned him when they had something on him, or almost on him. A man who had been under analysis by Wiley for more than a year had unfortunately gone too late to a physician for examination and been operated on, also too late, for a brain tumor. The Hollywood police had hinted, a little darkly, of what could happen to men who practiced medicine without a license.

Marley had provided the money for the irregular fee. Of that Wiley was quite certain. But the suggestion had actually been made, and the money actually handed over, by Peggy Belford—the reason given: Marley was too upset, too broken up, to do it himself.

The hypothesis: Peggy Belford had either known certainly, or guessed shrewdly, that Marley had killed his wife. The further hypothesis: She had later tried to cash in on guess or knowledge.

"Probably," Chris said, in her young voice, "he thought with mother out of the way, Peggy would marry him. She probably told him she would. The little—" She did not finish that, whether again at a signal from George Latham Heimrich could not tell.

"Also," Latham said, in a quiet voice, "she may have used her knowledge to pressure him into giving her parts. I guess it doesn't matter now, but we—all of us—a little underplayed that part of it. M. G. really had a thing about Peggy—a thing against her. I don't know why. So, between the devil and the deep blue sea."

There was, it was apparent, no lack of motive. It was also just as well that Marley, in a trap he did not recognize, had talked too much. The Hollywood police were of no mind, even now, to try to prove that, and explain how, Marley had given his wife an overdose of Nembutal.

Chris had fallen, inadvertently, into the trap set for Marley. (It is difficult to make an entirely selective trap.) Being told that Mrs. Faye—Heimrich closed his eyes briefly at the mention of Susan's name—had seen something, Chris had gone to look for the something, believing it would inculpate her stepfather. What Susan had seen might be something a man would miss. "After all, I'm a woman too," Chris said, with confidence.

"A baby," Latham said, softly. She did not appear to resent that.

And Heimrich suspected this might be because, perhaps only within recent hours, it had ceased to be true. She was, he thought, in the process of laying aside childish things, including childish crushes. Which would no doubt be a relief to Francis Dale.

She had run from the Collins house, down the path, to the scooter and away, because she had glimpsed Sergeant Forniss in the studio and thought him Marley and had had a chance to run. She had gone to Susan's house because, as she was passing it, she saw the unit's panel truck in the driveway.

"I thought, suppose he's gone there, instead of to the house," Chris said. "And went to see and—and he had. Trying to make Mrs. Faye think he was Francis. The rat."

"Yes," Heimrich said. "There was supposed to have been—" He stopped. There was no use going into that.

"She's mad, you know," Chris said. "Simply hopping. I mean angry mad."

"Now Miss Waggoner," Heimrich said, since that was another thing there was, then, no use in going into. "You'll remember what he said? Be prepared to testify?"

"Always," the girl said. "Any time, captain."

And he and Forniss would testify and Susan would. He did not doubt that; her anger would have nothing to do with that, whatever else it had to do with.

She must, he thought, feel this anger—this cold anger—because she had been used as bait. As secondary bait, which perhaps she did not fully realize. Under protection which—

Heimrich's mind stopped in its tracks. Which it was quite possible she did not know about. She had not waited to be told. And there did not seem to be any reason—except faith, which obviously she lacked—why she should guess that Trooper Crowley was on hand as bodyguard. Poor Crowley. And damn the dog.

[185]

For a second time he dialed the familiar number. "Hello," she said, coldly, far away. "Susan—" he said. And was hung up on.

Heimrich is slow to anger. But equanimity can be carried to extremes. He dialed once more. This time the telephone rang unanswered. Then Merton Heimrich lost his temper.

He needed a shave. He did not wait to shave. He needed coffee—at least coffee. He did not wait for coffee. He is a man who treats motor cars with gentleness, with respect. His car was jerked angrily out of its parking space, reversed with a snap which shook it. He drives with care on highways, and uses a siren only in emergencies. When another car looked like challenging him at The Corners Heimrich's siren snarled. And Heimrich, through the windshield, glared.

Loose gravel spat back under the car's churning wheels on the steep driveway to Susan's house. Susan was sitting on the terrace, on the chaise. A coffee cup was on a table beside her and she was smoking a cigarette. She looked up once, and looked away again, and did not move.

Heimrich went across the terrace with the fury and suddenness of a line squall. He stopped and stood over and glared down. She did not look at him—lay long and quiet on the chaise, motionless, incredibly distant.

"What do you mean hanging up on me?" Heimrich said—said very loudly. "What's the idea of hanging up on me?" She said nothing. "*Answer me!*" Heimrich said, his voice rough.

"Please go away," she said, in a voice from far off—from some distant cold of boredom. "Just go away. As far as you can go."

And, as if that ended it, she reached out toward the coffee cup on the table beside her.

The movement might have been a signal. She had no time to move farther; no time to touch the cup she reached toward. She seemed suddenly, inexplicably, to be flying through the air, her

wrists hurting. She landed on her feet, hard against the bulk of this
—who *was* this man? This man who had been so gentle—so too—

He took her by the shoulders. He shook her back and forth. Her
head waggled uncomfortably. She looked at a solid face she had
never seen before; into eyes she had never seen before.

"D-d-d-on't!" she said, the word shaken out of her. "You're hurting me."

"What's the matter with you?" he said, great anger in his voice.
But he did stop shaking her. "What the hell's the matter with you?"

"You'll break my neck," she said. "Is that what you want?"

But he was no longer shaking her. Her neck wasn't broken. The
only thing broken—the thing shattered—was her conception of this
big, now violent, man. A bump on a log? A man who thought she
would break?

"What do you mean hanging up on me?" he said again and shook
her again, but this time more lightly.

"Bait," she said. "That's what you used me for. Bait. Something
to be—*used*."

"You're crazy," Heimrich said. "What are you trying to do to us?"

It didn't make sense. It made the only sense there was in any of
this.

He held her off at arm's length and glared at her. He said, violently, *"Well?"*

"You saved my life once," she said. "All right. You saved it once.
So you thought that gave you a right to throw it away."

"You don't make sense," he said. But suddenly he took his hands
from her shoulders. "You weren't to be—risked. It—I didn't plan it
that way. You know that. You damn well know that."

"Why should I?" she said. "Tell me that. Why should I?"

"If you don't know that," Heimrich said, "what *do* you know?
Sure—things can slip. Always have. Always will. You want a glass
case? Cotton wool?"

"You—you're a clod," she said. "A *clod!*"

Which, also, didn't mean anything.

"I wasn't *afraid*," she said. "You think it was just that? Angry—you think I'm angry?"

"You," Heimrich said, "are damned right I do. Blowing up—no, freezing up—without finding anything out. Without knowing anything."

"Enough," she said. "I know enough. You didn't *care*. Didn't give a damn. I was—anything. An—an egg for an omelet. So, that's your way. That's your job. Now will you—will you get out of here? Just get—"

"Shut up!" Heimrich said. "Shut up!"

And then, with no more warning than she had had when she suddenly flew up off the chaise, she flew forward, her body bruisingly against his. "Shut up!" Heimrich said, somewhat wildly, and her lips hurt, bruised by his lips. Her lips which had waited—

She was, in an instant, again at arm's length.

"You hung up on me," he said, and again, but this time much more gently, shook her. "I won't have that. You hear me? Not any way. Not any way at all!" He shook her again. "Not *any* way," he said, once more, and glared down at her.

"I—" she said.

But she was back in his arms again; her lips silenced again. And —her arms were around him. Of all the things to happen. Why—this great *bully*. This— She clung to him. So he breaks my ribs, she thought, he breaks my ribs.

He did not. He picked her up. (But, she thought, I'm not that light. Not all that light.) He carried her to the chaise and sat her down on it, but now he was gentle. He sat down beside her. He looked at her. He seemed surprised at her, and at himself.

"Phew!" Susan Faye said, and then, briefly, he smiled.

"All the same," Merton Heimrich said, "you should have known there was—that there wasn't any risk planned. That I thought I had everything—taken care of."

"Well," she said.

"And," Heimrich said, "that I cared. So damn much that—" He shook his head. "You know," he said, "for a moment there I thought I was going to hit you." There was wonder in his tone.

She put a slender hand over his square hand.

"So did I," she said. "So did I, dear."

"It's a matter of trust," he said. "That's what—riled me up."

Which was, she thought, an inadequate way of putting it. But, perhaps not.

"God knows," he said, "I'm sorry things slipped. I—"

It was then that Colonel pushed open the screen door of the house and came out and sat on the terrace and looked at them.

"You," Heimrich said, to Colonel. "You damn fool dog."

"Merton," Susan Faye said, "I'm sorry I—I hung up. I won't again. I'll be very good and trust you and—and everything. But I do think that, now, you might tell me." She paused. "If you want to," she said. She couldn't deny herself that. He looked at her, suspiciously. Her face confirmed his suspicions.

"I don't ask that," he said. "Only that—that we both give each other the benefit of the doubt. Anyway, the chance." He looked at her steadily, for some seconds. "Always," he said, and she nodded her head.

"So—" Heimrich said. "Crowley's standing by and that dog of yours—"

She listened. A little line of worry appeared between her wide-set eyes, at the same time a slight smile appeared on her lips—her bruised lips.

"A damn fool thing," Heimrich said. "But—all kinds of damn fool things happen. We pretend things are orderly, go according to plans. And then some damn fool thing—"

[189]

"Poor Ray," she said. "He's all right?"

"Well," Heimrich said. "He's all right. But—he had quite an evening."

"More? More than Colonel?"

Heimrich smiled then.

"It's a little funny now," he said. "Crowley had a bad time all around. You see, he came to just before we—Latham and I—went in and—well, he saw Forniss by the car, where he was waiting just in case. And didn't recognize him, naturally enough. So he tried to come around behind him, planning to knock him off first—and—"

He paused.

"Well," he said, "Charlie's had a bit more experience and one thing and another. And there wasn't time for explanations, if he didn't want to be cracked with Crowley's gun. So— Charlie had to knock him out."

She said, "Oh!"

"As gently as possible," Heimrich said. "But—altogether a bad night for young Crowley."

"The poor boy," Susan said. "He—"

But she wasn't, so long as Raymond Crowley was all right, or going to be, really interested in Raymond Crowley. She looked at the solid man beside her, and looked with some wonder. How she could ever have thought—

And then, looking at him more carefully, she saw, for the first time, how inexpressibly tired his face was—how drawn. No sleep, or little sleep, she thought. But that, she thought, wasn't enough. Wasn't all of it; not nearly all of it.

How was I to know—she started to think, and checked herself. I did know, she thought. I just—just didn't go to enough trouble. I didn't know everything and never will and nobody ever does. (How amazingly strong he is!) But I should have known enough not—not to hang up on him. Give him so bad—

"Darling," Susan Faye said, "have you had any breakfast?"

He came back, apparently from some distance. His face came together again. He shook his head.

"No wonder," Susan Faye said, and started to get up. "I'll—"

He held out both hands to her. She shook her head, lightly, smiling.

"Breakfast," she said, firmly. "Breakfast first." He did not move to stop her. She took two steps toward the house—a slim young woman in a yellow summer dress, the morning light on her hair. She turned.

"Merton," Susan Faye said, "are you always going to be this grumpy before breakfast?"

Never, Heimrich thought, had he heard words more exquisitely lyrical.

"I like mine soft-boiled," Heimrich said, with great tenderness.